# ENDURING LOVE

## TONI SHILOH

Copyright © 2018 by Toni Shiloh

All rights reserved.

No part of this book may be reproduced in any form or by any electronic or mechanical means, including information storage and retrieval systems, without written permission from the author, except for the use of brief quotations in a book review.

Printed in the United States of America

First Printing: June 2018

Celebrate Lit Publishing

http://www.celebratelitpublishing.com/

ISBN-13

❦ Created with Vellum

## 1

There comes a point in every woman's life where she must decide what to believe: the truth of the past or the circumstances of the present. Belle Peterson chose the path of the present. It was an easy choice, considering her lingering scars. Not just physically, but the emotional ones she refused to show. Hopefully, her facial expressions wouldn't show the emotional ones now that she'd decided to forgo makeup and facial creams. Now a swipe of nude lip gloss from the local grocery was all that remained. Instead of dangling earrings, her earlobes remained bare. Her name-brand clothing had been traded in for a pair of scrubs and a cardigan, in case she got cold at work.

*Work.*

Belle bit the inside of her lip. She wasn't exactly sure how she felt about it. Never in her thirty years had she worked for the sole purpose of earning a living. However, her past actions had altered her future plans. Making a living as a nurse at Maple Run's Family Practice was a step on the right path. A godly path.

*Father, please be with me. I'm scared. Nervous. Worried I'll make a fool of myself. Please help me do my job to the best of my abilities and to the satisfaction of Dr. Kerrington.* "Amen," she whispered.

She headed for her small hatchback—a black Ford Focus. She hoped it made her seem unpretentious and conservative, a far cry from the convertible she'd traded in. Belle had shed no tears over the changes she'd implemented. It was for the best and a reminder that she'd willingly left her old life behind. No matter what others may think.

Heat blasted from the car's vent, finally thawing her fingers and toes. When would she be used to the frigid cold of Virginia's winter season? Unfortunately, winter didn't officially start for another twenty-three days. But who was counting? In a season where people 'decked the halls' and sang with holiday cheer, that same joy was oddly absent in her life.

Everywhere she turned reminded her of the countdown to Christmas. Normally, she'd have bought tons of gifts by now. This year, she'd simply thank her Heavenly Father for new beginnings. It was the only measure of comfort she had. That and her new job.

A small smile graced her lips as she headed to work. Today would be her very first day using her bachelor's degree in nursing, despite having received it four years after graduating high school. She'd never put it to use. Hadn't been allowed to.

*"Pretty faces have no need for jobs, Belle."*

Chill bumps spread down her arms, raising the tiny hairs as a memory threatened to surface. No need to look back. *"This one thing I do,"* she murmured. *"Forgetting those things which are behind, and reaching forth unto those things which are before."* The words of Philippians echoed softly in the quiet car. She'd taped the verse on the steering wheel of her car as a reminder to not look back. God had made her a new creation.

*Focus on the present, Belle. Focus.*

In a matter of minutes, she pulled into the family practice parking lot. A month ago, she had applied for the job after finding the small town of Maple Run, Virginia a perfect place to start over. Doctor Kerrington had been kind but concise when they did the interview over Skype. Unfortunately, her physical scars had been evident at the time. The doctor had promised not to share her health history with anyone, and he only knew a snippet of what she'd been through.

*Push it back, don't think about it.*

Hopefully, Dr. Kerrington would maintain professionalism at work. Since he was pushing toward seventy and had a quiver full of grandchildren, she prayed it meant he would be an honorable man. Too many weren't.

Opening the back door, Belle paused, her breath hovering in the air before disappearing in the warmth of the office. *Time to start a new chapter.*

Taking a deep breath to steady her nerves, Belle crossed the threshold and headed for the locker room to store her coat and bag. The office had a chill in the air but was still warmer than outside. Still, she kept her white cardigan on, deciding it looked more presentable with her navy-blue scrubs. Professional even.

After locking everything up, she headed for Dr. Kerrington's office. She paused outside his closed office door. Her pulse skittered as nerves overtook her. *What am I doing?* Why did she ever think she could be a nurse?

*You have to do this, Belle. You have no other options.*

She closed her eyes and exhaled, imagining the doubts being pushed out. It was now or never. Time to grow up and be the woman God was showing her she could be. Before she could change her mind, she knocked on the door.

"Come in."

She twisted the knob and entered the room.

"Ah, Belle. Good morning." Doctor Kerrington rose from his desk. His white lab coat shone brightly against his pale blue shirt; his stethoscope laid across the back of his neck.

She stared, stunned. Not because of the good doctor but because of the handsome man who had risen in her presence. Her brain short-circuited. "I'm sorry," she stammered. "I didn't realize someone else was in here."

"Oh, no worries." The doctor waved a hand, blue veins prominent in his pale skin. His bushy white eyebrows lifted with cheer. "This is Micah Campbell, our PA. Micah, meet Belle Peterson, our newest nurse."

*He* was the physician assistant? *Oy.*

Micah took a step forward and held out a hand in greeting.

Belle took in his appearance, noting how his dark complexion seemed to gleam in the office light. Of course, it could have been the shine reflecting off his bald head that captivated her. And boy, did bald look good on him. It seemed to emphasize the black mustache and goatee, perfectly lined against his rich dark skin as well as his lips.

*Pull yourself together. You promised not to think that way about the opposite sex anymore.*

But how could she ignore his black pearl eyes? Or the way his lashes seemed to frame them? It should be a crime for a man to have perfect eyelashes like that. *Belle!* Right, she'd focus on his age. Yes, that was safe. The PA appeared to be mid-thirties. She'd ignore how his ears fit perfectly against the sides of his head or how full his lips were. *Again.*

Tentatively, she reached out her hand and shook his. Chills raced up her arm at the contact.

*No, no, no.* She would *not* be attracted. "Nice to meet you." She added a tad bit of frost into her tone as a defense mechanism. She was here as a professional, not some medical groupie.

"Likewise," he said with a dip of his head. His lips pulled up in a slight smile.

"Soup is going to show you around." Doctor Kerrington clapped a hand on Micah's shoulder.

"Soup?" Her eyes darted between the two of them.

"Army nickname." Micah shrugged, giving her a rueful glance.

"Oh, because of Campbell?"

"Yes, ma'am."

Doctor Kerrington chuckled. "Cracks me up every time. The

kids are too young to get it, but it makes the adults feel more comfortable." The doctor took hold of her hand. "Belle, we're so glad you could join the practice. If you have any questions at all, just ask. Anna, one of the other nurses, will be coming in this afternoon for her shift. Until then, you're on your own for the morning watch."

*Oh, Lord, please don't let me fail.* "Sounds good, sir."

"Oh, call me Doc or Dr. K like everyone else."

"Okay."

"Micah," Doc said, turning toward the man in question. "Could you give us a second? I'll meet you out in the hall shortly."

"Sure, Doc," Micah said. He turned toward her. "Nice to meet you again, Belle."

She dipped her head, too worried to speak. What did the doctor want to talk about?

"Have a seat, Belle." He gestured toward a blue-cushioned chair as he sat down across from her. "I wanted to know how you're feeling? Are you good to work now?" Concern filled his cornflower blue eyes.

Her insides clenched. Why did he have to go digging into her past? She just wanted a fresh start. "I'm fine, Dr. K. All healed."

His brow wrinkled. "What about emotionally?"

"God's getting me through it." He was the only one who could. Without His love, she'd be destitute.

Relief flooded the doctor's face, softening the angular nose and lines marking his age. His eyes softened. "Good to hear. Maple Run has a great church community if you're interested."

"Thank you." Was she? She'd never belonged to a church before.

"Well, I just wanted to check. I have an open door policy around here, Belle. Don't be a stranger." He grinned, folding his hands across his belly.

"Thank you."

She got up and walked out. Hopefully, that would be the last of his questions. How could she move on if others were intent on dragging her back? Granted, he was the only one in Maple Run that had a glimpse of her past. Now that he was assured the scars were healed, maybe she could truly do so. It was time to step into the life God offered her.

Micah pulled up the day's patient list on his office laptop. Hmm, they still had openings remaining. Hopefully, it meant today wouldn't be so taxing. However, since the winter season was upon them, there were bound to be walk-ins coming in to complain of flu-like symptoms. Thankfully, his vaccinations were up-to-date, a must in the medical career field.

As the list of names populated his laptop screen, a different image occupied his mind: Belle Peterson. Despite the lack of makeup and large scrubs hanging on her slender frame, beauty radiated from her. Cat-shaped eyes, high cheek bones, and full pink lips begged for a second, more in-depth glance. The way her brown eyes sparkled against her copper skin tone didn't hurt either. Too bad her personality was about as warming as damp socks. The ice in her introduction irritated him to his core. Not because he thought her rude. No, he knew her type. One of those beautiful women who assumed a friendly smile from the opposite sex meant he *had* to be hitting on her.

He'd had enough of conceited women who thought they could trample all over men. Belle Peterson didn't have to worry. Her message had been received loud and clear. He'd do his best to steer clear of her but still treat her professionally. At thirty-eight and having been through countless years of working with difficult soldiers, he knew how to toe the line.

From the corner of his eye, he saw movement. Mimi Page, the officer manager, entered and turned on the waiting room lights before unlocking the glass front door. Outside, the trees dipped under the weight of the wind. Yep, they would definitely be seeing people suffering from colds today.

"Morning, Mimi." It felt weird calling his elder by her first name, but she insisted.

The older woman whirled around, her brown bohemian skirt flaring out. Her sweater sleeves were pushed up around her elbows and her ivory skin looked flushed. She always claimed she was hot, but still continued to wear sweaters.

"Good morning, Soup." She opened the half door behind the front desk. "Did you meet Belle?"

"I did." He leaned against the back wall that formed the little alcove.

"Isn't she just the cutest thing? Real sweet too."

It took all his past military training to school his features. Did they meet the same woman? "She seems nice," he hedged.

"Well of course she's nice." She met his gaze, her reddish blonde eyebrows hiking upward. "Doc doesn't hire mean people. We're a family practice, Micah."

Her dramatic voice arched high and low, entertaining him as she spoke. Her theatrical background showcased in her speech and movements. Why she ended up as an officer manager for a family practice instead of ruling the theater scene was beyond him.

"You make sure to show her the ropes." Mrs. Page huffed as she placed a hand on her hip. "And maybe show her around town. She's new here and doesn't know anyone."

"I'm quite new myself, Mimi." He'd only lived in Maple Run for six months. The offer to work with Doc had been an answered prayer.

"True, but I know you're an explorer."

*More like homebody.* "Not really. I like to stick close to home."

"But you were in the military." Shock widened her eyes, the green color darkening with her emotion.

Why did people always assume those in the military liked to

travel? He knew more military men and women who chose to stick close to home instead of traveling the world. "I was. Saw a few countries, but I prefer being close to home."

When he became a PA and hung up his Army hat, he'd happily joined the civilian lifestyle. It was odd being a civilian, but a normal he was learning to appreciate.

"Regardless, you're a good guy, so I know you'll show Belle around town."

"That's not necessary, Mrs. Page."

Micah turned at the sound of Belle's soft voice. It seemed to hover in the air like the sound of angels. He snorted. The holiday season had made him a little kooky.

She stood there, arms wrapped around her waist, as if trying to keep him away.

*Message received.*

"You can call me, Mimi, dear. Besides, you don't know anyone in town. At least let Micah take you to lunch." Mrs. Page looked at him expectantly.

*Lunch.*

For the first time that morning, a genuine grin took place on his face. "We can go to The Maple Pit," he offered. "Best food for miles."

Belle tilted her chin, her pert nose aiming for the ceiling. "No, thank you."

*Translation: not on your life.*

Irritation filled him. He didn't want to take her to lunch, but he did want to please Mrs. Page. "Belle, it's not a problem. I can promise you, you'll love the food *and* the people there."

She bit her lip, indecision crossing her face. Shock filled his being. She looked approachable. Likeable even.

"Are you sure?" Her voice was full of caution.

"Yes. It'll be fun." *I hope.*

Having lunch with a woman putting out the back-off vibe wasn't his idea of an enjoyable lunch. He glanced at Mrs. Page, who nodded with approval. The older woman's grin lit up her face, Cheshire-cat style.

"All right. Thank you. I'll join you." Her words were stilted and laced with frost.

*And she's back.*

"Fantastic!" Mrs. Page clapped her hands together. "You'll love The Pit's food, Belle. I'd eat there every day if I wasn't trying to watch my waist do anything but expand."

Micah chuckled. "Fishing, Mimi?"

"I am if you're catching." She fluffed up her bun and fluttered her eyelashes.

He laughed outright. "Your figure is flattering on you. Go eat at The Pit."

"Well, you're just too kind, Soup. However, I brought a salad to enjoy. You two go on and have fun." She wiggled her fingers at them, looking pleased as could be.

A grimace passed over Belle's face...then again, it could have been a smile.

*Oh, joy. What a start to the week, Lord. Is this what I get for praying for patience?*

Because the Lord knew he'd need it to get through the rest of the day, especially lunch. He looked at Belle, trying to gather his thoughts. "The office closes from noon to one. We can go to lunch then, if that's acceptable with you?" He tried to add warmth to his voice, but the lady seriously annoyed him.

"Noon's fine." She looked at him, then the laptop. "What time is the first patient coming?"

*Subject changed.* "The appointment is in fifteen minutes."

The front door chimed.

"There you go." He gestured toward the door.

"I'll get to work then."

He watched her as she headed for the triage room. Yep, today was going to be an interesting day.

## 2

Belle looked around The Maple Pit. *No, the locals call it The Pit.* Interesting name for a restaurant shaped like a barn. She'd expected an interior full of picnic tables and cheap checkered tablecloths. Instead, the oak tables were covered in cream-colored linens and flower-filled mason jars adding a touch of home. It was rustic but chic at the same time.

A pretty redhead led them to a table for two. Belle glanced longingly at the bar. If they ate there, maybe it wouldn't feel like they were on a date. *You're not on a date.* A breath of air whooshed out. Her mind knew that, but her old self was so used to being wined and dined that it was hard not to adopt the behavior she'd normally exhibit. The behavior Garrett had encouraged.

Flirtatious and coy.

She'd used them so often the tools became second nature. And although Micah didn't want anything from her, the nature Garrett had shaped and molded, begged for reentry. It was scary how her old self desperately tried to take back control as she attempted to adopt a lifestyle of righteousness.

*You'll help me, right, Lord?*

Belle sat down, thankful Micah didn't hold her chair out. She glanced around. "I take it this place is a local favorite?" She stared at Micah hoping he'd accept her olive branch of light conversation.

*That a girl, no reason to be completely rude.* The way the hairs on her arms stood at attention at his nearness wasn't his fault. Surely, it would react the same way around any good-looking man. She'd just be sure to send a message of not interested to keep herself on the straight and narrow.

"Locals and beyond. My friend's fiancée is part owner."

"Cool." She stared at her silverware. Her mind had no idea what to say when not in flirt mode.

"What brings you to Maple Run, Belle?"

"I, uh...the job." She met Micah's gaze, resting her folded arms against the table. "Doctor K was kind enough to offer me the position so..." She shrugged.

"Now you're here."

"That's right. And you? I thought I heard you mention you haven't lived here long."

"I haven't." He folded his arms, placing them on the table.

Was he mocking her? Or did he rest his arms on the table for comfort?

"I recently received my PA license and Doc hired me. I've been working for him now for six months. I'm from Bethesda, Maryland which isn't too far from here."

"Oh, congratulations."

More silence. *Terrific.* Before she could bang her head against the table, a tall statuesque woman stopped in front of their table.

"Hey, Micah, back so soon?"

"Ha." He grinned, his white teeth flashing.

It really was a shame that the man was so good-looking.

"Delaney, this is Belle." He gestured toward her. "She's new, so of course I had to introduce her to the best place to eat."

Delaney smiled at her, offering a hand. "Nice to meet you, Belle."

"You too." Her lips lifted in response, thankful for the genuine warmth she saw in Delaney's eyes.

"Are you a light eater?" Delaney asked.

In the past, she'd always been conscious of impressing the opposite sex. Now, she had to be sure to repel them. "I like to eat." And she really did.

"Then I suggest the maple fried chicken with two sides."

"Maple? Fried?" Both her eyebrows rose in one accord. She'd never been able to arch one at a time.

Micah grinned. "The chicken's out of this world, Belle."

"Okay, I'll have that." She ignored the flutters that appeared at his grin. *God, I could use your help. I don't want to be attracted to men—or him. Especially him.* Office relationships were a no-no.

"Where's Luke?" Micah asked.

"He should be coming in for lunch in a few. I'll tell him to come over."

"Tell who to come over?" A deep voice asked.

Belle peered around Delaney to see a tall man with a golden complexion and dreamy blue eyes step up to the table. He kissed Delaney's forehead. "Hey, darlin.'"

Delaney's lips curled into a sappy-looking grin.

The man nodded to Micah. "How's it going, Soup?"

Micah stood and gave him a back clap. "Good, Crusoe. Let me introduce you to our new nurse." He gestured toward her once more. "Luke, this is Belle. Belle, this is my friend, Luke, Delaney's fiancé."

Surprise filtered through her. An interracial couple in the deep South would turn heads. Here, though, everyone seemed to be one big happy family. "Nice to meet you."

They shook hands and she sighed in relief when no spark appeared. *Thank you.*

"Nice to meet you too, Belle."

He had a country accent, not so much Southern, but there was a twang.

"Where are you from?" The words popped out before she could recall them.

"Texas." His lips curved up and grooves appeared on the sides of his mouth. They were too deep to be dimples but just as cute.

And not a single note of desire tinged through her. Was she cured? Had God truly recreated her into a new being? "Whereabouts?"

"West Texas. You been?"

"Just to Dallas." For a conference. Not that she attended the conference. No, she'd merely been arm candy when required.

"Go Cowboys," Luke responded.

"Boo," she and Micah said in unison.

Surprise filtered across Micah's face. "You like football?" he asked.

"Who doesn't?"

"Me." Delaney offered a sheepish smile as she turned to go. "I'll put your order in right away."

With a wave good-bye, Luke followed her.

Silence descended, bringing the awkwardness back.

"I can't believe you like football," Micah said, leaning back into his chair.

"Carolina Panthers." She shrugged like it wasn't a big deal, but her insides quaked. Experience taught her that guys didn't want to hear about a woman's likes and dislikes. Yet, he seemed genuinely interested.

"Panthers, huh? I'm a Ravens fan all the way."

"We all have flaws."

A shocked bark of laughter tore from his lips. "Apparently, there's more to you than meets the eye, Miss Peterson."

"Like the fact that I'm not a transformer?" When a flash of laughter filled his eyes, she didn't know whether to be irritated or laugh with him. "No one is as they appear, Mr. Campbell."

"I'm beginning to see that."

Belle shoved her hands between her legs, trying to keep them still and maintain her cool façade underneath his piercing gaze. She didn't need him or want him looking too deep. Why had she said that? The last thing she needed was for him to decide she had secrets for him to uncover. "Mr. Campbell..."

"Please, call me Micah or Soup. We're colleagues, not strangers."

"I just met you."

He sighed. "Continue, please."

She bit her lip. "I just wanted to say, what you see is what you get. I'm not into games." She paused, wondering if she should vocalize her thoughts. *Couldn't hurt.* "And I'm not interested in dating."

"I see." Micah slowly nodded. "If it makes you feel better, I don't date either."

Sweet relief flooded her being. So, he hadn't been hinting. Didn't even want to date. Her eyes smarted. It had all been in her head.

"However, I seriously doubt that there aren't hidden layers. Everyone has secrets."

Was it his imagination or did her face pale? Micah tried to study her without being obvious. Her sleek bob fell just below her ears, accenting the stunning shape of her eyes. She really was a natural beauty. Not a hint of makeup—except the shine on her lips. The simplicity of it captivated him. Maybe his quick judgment of her would prove false. When Belle spoke to Delaney, genuine kindness exuded from her. An open smile had graced her full lips, making her dark brown eyes sparkle. She even talked to Luke with a warmth he'd yet to be graced with.

So, what was it? Did she just turn on the frost with men she worked with? *No,* that made no sense. She was more than cordial with Doc. It had to be him, but why? What did he do...say?

"Do you have secrets?" Her voice interrupted his thoughts.

"Sure." He shrugged. *Like what?*

"Do you share them with strangers?" Her fingers mindlessly twirled her fork between her fingers.

He stared at her. *What was with this woman?* Despair seemed to be her second face. Happy and cordial one minute, somber and depressed the next. "Not usually."

"Hmm, I see." She put her fork down and stared straight into his eyes. "Then why do you think I should reveal my life story to you?"

"Whoa, that's not what I meant."

"Really?" Both of her perfectly arched eyebrows raised up.

A hint at the vanity he thought she possessed or did she once sport a unibrow?

"Sounded that way to me."

"No, I'm just saying the phrase, 'what you see is what you get' is a falsehood. No one shows everything. There's always something hidden. Always."

His fist tightened at his side. He'd learned that the hard way. People expected honesty and goodness from a pretty face, but good-looking people were often the most deceptive.

"That's a surprising observation coming from a man." Her mouth twisted in bitterness.

*Another layer.* "Why is that? You think men don't show their true selves?"

"No," she snorted. "They're worse than women."

"Oh, come on. Women are the queens of two-faced behavior. Smile and say 'yes,' but are vehemently shaking their head 'no' on the inside. It's no wonder there's so much grief between the sexes."

"Caused by men."

"No, I don't think so, sister." He slid back away from the table, done with the conversation. Unfortunately, Delaney walked up with their plates.

*Lord, I need that divine patience here.* Something about Belle made him lose his cool and he didn't like it. He considered himself to be a nice person, but her attitude made him forget his desire to be more Christ-like.

"Fried chicken for you." Delaney smiled at Belle, who responded in kind.

"And loaded baked potato soup for you, Micah." The smell of the soup wafted over him, bringing a calm that had previously been absent.

"Thanks, Dee."

"Sure, can I get y'all anything else?" Dee smiled at the both of them.

"Luke rubbing off on you?" He grinned at her choice of slang.

"Nah. I said it before I knew him. Besides, he says I don't say it like a Texan. Whatever that means." She rolled her eyes. "Enjoy."

He watched as Belle chewed her food with abandonment. *Amazing.* He'd never seen a woman eat without concern for her weight. With her slim figure, he thought for sure she'd eat like a bird. Yet, she dove into the chicken like she hadn't eaten breakfast.

Then again, maybe she didn't.

*Stop thinking about her and eat.*

But he couldn't. Her back-and-forth behavior consumed his thoughts. He barely tasted the tantalizing flavors in the soup. Being here with Belle rendered it tasteless—almost as bad as having sawdust in his mouth.

Her body moved around in a happy rhythm as she ate her two chicken legs before moving on to the mac-n-cheese. His eyes captured her every movement. She made it abundantly clear how much she enjoyed her food.

"This is so good."

"Their mac-n-cheese is my favorite." In the summer, they offered seafood choices to add to it. His mouth watered thinking about the crab version.

"I never would have thought to add bacon to mac-n-cheese."

"They love maple bacon around here. In case you hadn't figured it out, they like maple everything."

Belle chuckled, looking carefree for the first time, since their conversation went down that bitter road. "It works, but I see running in my near future."

"You run?" That was surprising. She didn't seem like the type.

"How else can you stay healthy if you don't exercise?" Curiosity widened her eyes.

He'd never seen that shade of brown before. It was like mahogany. Or maybe the cherry desk in his home library. He blinked, looking down into his soup bowl. *Why am I looking at her eyes?*

"Micah?"

"Sure," he refocused his thoughts. "We all need exercise. You just don't look like you do." His face warmed, realizing it sounded like a backhanded compliment.

"That's why I exercise." She smirked and took another bite of her food.

His mind couldn't keep up. Belle Peterson was a conundrum. Part of him wanted to examine every facet and explore her responses. The other half knew when you got too close to fire, you got burned.

*Neither of us wants to date. Nothing to worry about.*

Still, his brain had a niggling feeling he was simply fooling himself. Micah never imagined a lifetime with his ex-wife, but he ended up marrying her anyway with that goal in mind. *Look how that turned out.*

No, beautiful women couldn't be trusted. If he ever dated, it would be someone average-looking. A person grounded in faith and intent on keeping God first. *If* a woman could do that, maybe he could be reassured she'd have his best interests at heart. Until then, dating was off limits.

## 3

Boredom attacked Belle's sanity with slow, well-placed thumps to her brain. The cream-colored walls of her apartment stared at her, mocking her with their emptiness. She'd taken a minimalist approach to decorating, going with the bare necessities for furniture as well. Now, regret filled her as the blank walls seemed to smother her. Why hadn't she at least bought a TV?

Granted, she'd never had the time to watch it before. Plus, Garrett...no, she wouldn't think about him. Suffice it to say, the opportunity to watch TV had never presented itself. Perhaps that's what she should do. Go out and buy one. Exactly where did one go to do that? She had no idea, but it was time to find out.

Belle grabbed her car keys and her over-the-shoulder purse. Perhaps there would be an appliance store nearby. Maple Run was small, but there were other towns nearby, if one didn't mind the drive. She pulled up the GPS app on her cell.

After a half-hour drive, she found the store that claimed it sold televisions and headed inside. Funny, how she couldn't remember the way she used to spend her time. Garrett had—

*No, no, no. Stop thinking of that evil...*

A groan of frustration rolled in her throat. She wished God

would wipe one's memory away when He blessed people with a new self. It would make life so much easier. *Don't you think, Lord?*

No answer.

Not that she really expected one. He never gave her an audible reply, but at times, she felt warmth in her heart. Belle continued to the back of the store and stopped as she came to the electronics area. TVs lined the wall, each vying for her attention. Some were small, others massive. She rubbed her temple. This should be simple, right? Just pick one and go home.

Then what?

"Need some help?"

A man with a store-issued polo grinned at her. Interest exuded from his pores.

*Great.* "Um, I was just thinking about buying a TV."

"I can *definitely* help with that." He winked at her as if his comment hadn't been obvious enough.

Should she ask someone else to help her?

"What size are you looking for?"

"Just something to watch some shows on. It doesn't have to be as big as that one." She pointed to the biggest one and bit her lip. Then again, it might be neat to watch the football games on something that big.

She hadn't been able to watch a game at home in so long. "Well, maybe that size is okay. How much is it?"

He listed off a price that made her purse shudder.

"Okay, so definitely not that big."

The man chuckled. "You know I get a discount. I could be persuaded to use it." He ran a finger down her arm.

*Ew.* She stepped back. "No, thank you." In a different time and place, she might have responded in kind, if Garrett thought a benefit would come of it. But that was before Christ had cleaned her.

"I'll make it worth your while."

"No." She shook her head. "You know what? Never mind." *Time to go.* She turned, ready to bolt.

"Hold up." He reached for her, his hands wrapping around her wrist.

Blind panic seized her. Her throat closed at the implications. She couldn't move, couldn't speak.

"Let her go."

*Micah.* She turned, her bones sagging in relief. His name fell from her lips like a benediction.

The ferocious look on his face scared her, until she realized it was directed at the employee. "Let. Her. Go."

The man dropped her arm, hands held up in surrender. "All yours, my man." He threw one more leer her way and sauntered off.

Her right wrist ached where his touch had seared into her skin. She rubbed it, noting the feel of the puckered scar. Inconspicuously, she pulled her sleeve down, then wrapped her arms around her stomach. "Thank you."

Micah nodded. "You okay?"

"Yes." *No.*

"You sure?"

No, but she wasn't going to tell him that. "I'm fine. Figures, I'd have a problem." The bitterness swirled through her, threatening to drag her down. She just wanted to buy a stupid TV. Why did men always look at her and demand a price?

"Do you need help?" Micah slid his hands into his pockets and rocked back slightly on the balls of his feet.

"I just wanted to buy a TV."

"You don't own one?" An arched eyebrow made its presence.

"How do you do that?"

He froze. "Do what?"

"Arch your eyebrow? I can never do it. I had to tweeze them this way." She motioned to her eyebrows and the flawless arched look that had taken years to perfect. They were the only thing she kept of her old look.

A chuckle rumbled from his chest. "Good ol' DNA."

"Lucky."

A bemused expression filled Micah's face. "How about I help you?" He gestured toward the wall with his head. "What kind of TV do you want?"

"One to watch football on, but not one that will break my bank."

"Fair enough."

For the next few minutes, Micah went through TVs, asking her various questions she would have never even thought of. Finally, she picked one that could be mounted on the wall or displayed on a stand.

"Do you need a stand or are you going to mount it?"

"Um...I don't know?" Her voice rose with each word. Was there any place in her apartment for the TV to sit?

"Let me look at the box, maybe it comes with a mount." He bent over the box. "No mount, but it has its own stand. You'll still need something for it to sit on. Do you have a book shelf, TV stand, or coffee table? Something to set it on?" He stared at her expectantly.

His eyes were gorgeous. The color of a black pearl.

"Belle?"

She blinked. Right, they were talking about stands. "I can use a coffee table."

"You can also buy a stand. I'm sure they sell some that won't break the bank."

"All right."

After making her purchases, Micah pushed the cart to her car. He stopped abruptly when he saw her car.

"You expect this stuff to fit in that?" He pointed at her hatchback.

"What's wrong with it? The TV isn't that big."

"Yes, but the stand is awkward."

"I'll fold down the passenger seat."

He peered in the car. "That'll work. Are you able to get it inside your place or should I follow you?"

A man in her apartment? Not on her life. But did she have the muscles to get it inside? She bit her lip trying to decide what to do. "If you can just carry it up the stairs, I can do the rest." She stared at the TV, refusing to meet his gaze. She didn't want him to think she was flirting.

"I can do that. Then I'll leave and be out of your hair. Promise." His voice lowered as a solemnness overtook it.

She looked up and read the sincerity in his gaze. But how could she trust it? Men could show whatever they wanted to.

"I promise, Belle."

"Okay," she nodded. *Please, don't let him hurt me, Lord.*

Except she didn't know if that was a benediction against physical or emotional harm.

Anger coursed through him. Micah's hands involuntarily tightened around the steering wheel as he followed Belle back to Maple Run. Someone had put his hands on her. And not the slimy employee who had ogled her like a fifty-cent special at the gas station. No, the fear that flashed in her eyes when that joker grabbed her wrist proved it wasn't her first experience with being manhandled.

His jaw flexed at the thought. What kind of man would dare lay hands on a woman? There was no acceptable reason on earth for a man to abuse his strength. God gave woman to man to be protected, not used as a punching bag.

*Breathe, Campbell.*

*1...2...3...*

Failure. The anger still felt hot in his veins, speeding his pulse and skyrocketing his blood pressure to dangerous proportions.

*Lord, please help me show her that I would never hurt her. I know she's scared to let me in her apartment. Please comfort her and heal her emotional scars.*

Could that be the reason she moved to Virginia? Did she still have someone chasing after her or was he safely behind bars? The need to ask her swelled, and he exhaled, pushing it down. It would take time to build trust. No way could he ask her if she'd been abused in a normal, everyday conversation.

*Patience, Campbell.*

A groan of frustration tore free. It always came back to patience. The Lord would ask him to wait, and he'd readily agree. Then days, months, sometimes even years passed by, and his skin would itch with impatience.

Only he knew what lack of perseverance led to. He had the divorce paperwork to remind him of the error of his ways. He'd often wondered if the blame rested solely on him. Was his love not the enduring kind? Or had he been suffocating with his affections?

*Wait on the Lord; be of good courage, and he shall strengthen thine heart; wait, I say, on the Lord.*

He exhaled as the verse scrolled in his mind. It was time to commit to patience. Building trust with a battered woman was too important. Time could *not* be rushed, not if he could help it. He pressed the brake, slowing as Belle pulled into a long driveway next to a blue Victorian.

Instead of driving all the way to the back, she stopped the car near the sidewalk leading to the front porch. He exited his SUV. "I thought you lived in an apartment."

"You ever see any apartment buildings in Maple Run?"

"No," he said slowly.

She laughed. "The owner turned the house into four apartments. I'm on the top floor." She pointed upward.

"Oh."

Belle raised the hatchback and stepped back. He reached for the TV and paused. The scent of vanilla drifted toward him. It reminded him of the winter season and cozying up in front of a fire.

*Not with Belle Peterson, you're not.*

He exhaled and lifted the box. "Lead the way."

His stomach tightened as he thought of all the reasons why developing anything past a professional relationship was a bad idea.

*She's been hurt.*

*You don't trust women.*

*You're not even sure you like her.*

Well, that wasn't entirely true. He didn't *want* to like her. A beautiful face had been his ruin in the past. Weren't you supposed to learn from your mistakes?

He slowed as he reached the top step in front of her place.

"You can set it down here."

Micah looked around the box to see Belle point to a spot near the front door. After he sat it down he looked at her. "I'll go get the other box. Can you lock the car door from up here so you don't have to go back downstairs?"

She nodded.

"Good, when you see me, lock it." He headed back downstairs without waiting for a response.

Self-preservation began to kick in. He needed to get out of there before his impulsiveness added another regret to his list. Now wasn't the time to insert himself where he wasn't needed. Even if it pained him to think of her putting up the TV all by herself. After going back up the stairs, he put the box next to the first one.

Her front door remained closed.

"All set." He looked up and for a moment, sadness marred her features. His insides screamed to offer comfort. "If you need anything else, just let me know tomorrow at work. I'm sure I can help."

"Actually…" she paused, biting her lip in nervousness.

He tried not to stare. "Yes?"

"How does cable work?"

An eyebrow arched before he could stop it. She didn't know about cable? "You have to get a provider, so that you can watch shows. However, since you just bought a smart TV, you could use your internet connection and use a service like Netflix or Hulu."

"I don't have the internet."

His mouth dropped open. He couldn't help it. How did a woman her age not have internet? "But you have a smart phone."

"I use data through my carrier." She shrugged. "Besides, I don't use it that much. Just for emergency purposes."

She had no friends to call? Family? Wasn't everyone on social media these days? Her layers became more complex by the minute. "If you give me your cell number, I'll text you the local provider info. They can get you hooked up for cable and internet."

Indecision warred on her face, deepening her mahogany eyes.

"Or I can write it on a note pad."

"Just a second." She headed inside, closing the door behind her. She came back and handed him a magnetic notepad and pen. And the door remained closed at all times.

Yep, she'd definitely been hurt before. Micah wrote the provider information down and handed her the pad. "See you tomorrow."

"Thank you for the help." She swallowed and glanced down. "Especially at the store."

"Anytime."

Without another word, he turned and headed down the stairs. All the while, his mind screamed at him to return. To assure her it wasn't her fault the slime bucket had crossed the line. But if he went back, he'd destroy the trust he wanted to build.

Belle had to believe he would fulfill his promise. With that in mind, Micah hopped into his SUV and headed home. In a few minutes, his craftsman style house came into view. The gray siding seemed to blend in with the winter's landscape. The white columns framing the porch and adding to the face of the home. When the snow came, it would make a picturesque scene. The stately gray against the pure white. It was one of the things he loved about the place—masculine but still showcased nature's beauty.

Weariness dragged him down as he headed through the door that connected the garage to the house. He strolled down the hallway, toward the kitchen.

His African grey parrot squawked, "Hello," as he came into view. The bird cage was situated in the corner of the living room. Thanks to the open floor plan, his friend could see him in the kitchen.

"Hey, Noodle. It's me." Micah paused, opening the refrigerator to look for some fruit.

"Hungry?"

"Not me, Noodle. You hungry?"

"Noodle hungry."

He put some cantaloupe in a stainless-steel bowl, and then walked toward the cage to feed his parrot.

"Thank you," Noodle squawked.

"You're welcome."

Noodle cocked his head to the side and stared at him. It was as if the bird could sense his inner turmoil. Because his insides *were* battered. This morning, he'd been so sure of what type of person Belle was. Now...well, he had no clue what to think.

Her back-off vibes made more sense. She probably saw him as a threat. It would explain why Mrs. Page thought Belle was nice. Probably also why the Doc didn't scare her. Who would be scared of a seventy-plus-year-old-family doctor?

But him? He could be imposing.

He worked out regularly, courtesy of his military background.

Despite hanging up his Army hat, his body was still used to conditioning. He enjoyed keeping fit, as evident in his home gym. Micah sank into his recliner as the image of Belle's frightened eyes branded into his memory.

"Aw, man, I forgot the speakers." He slapped his thigh in frustration.

One look at that suggestive look on that smarmy employee's face had erased the reason he went to the store in the first place. His surround-sound speaker had blown while he'd been watching TV earlier. All he wanted was to replace the thing. Now, he'd have to make another trip, but not tonight. *Too overwhelmed, Lord.*

## 4

Her first week of work flew by. In the beginning, she'd felt insecure of her skills. Every second Belle wondered if Dr. K would regret his decision to hire her. Slowly but surely, her training kicked in and her mind remembered what to look for. Thankfully, she'd taken a nursing refresher course before she started her job hunt. It turned out to be a life saver.

Now, she looked forward to her first weekend off. Her first week as a bona fide adult had been a success. No one called the shots but her. No one dictated what she could or couldn't do, or what she could watch. Of course, there were too many options available on TV now that she had cable. Fortunately, she discovered a show that flipped houses. It captivated her. There were so many endless opportunities to make a home your own. For a moment, she wished she could buy her own place instead of renting.

Despite the addition of TV, boredom hounded her. She was in desperate need of a hobby. Hence the reason she found herself in Maple Run's only craft store, run by a Mrs. Adams. The older woman had greeted her with the warmth of a long-time friend.

Oddly enough, Mrs. Adams had been helping Mimi, from work, with a quilting pattern.

Weird how easily you could run into someone you knew in town. That wouldn't have happened so easily in Charlotte. Then again, the circles she frequented had been filled with people she knew. It was one of the reasons she fled after...

She sighed, absently rubbing the scar on her right wrist. The one that took almost three months to heal. The scars were her own fault. Even though she hated them, they served as a reminder to never go down the wrong path again. Righteous living only from here on out.

*And steer clear of men!*

Some men were evil just because. Others weren't thinking with their brains when stupidity took over. Shoving the pressing memories back, Belle headed for the yarn section. She'd always admired the scarves and socks people made. Didn't they use a crochet needle to make them? Or was that knitting? She had no clue.

"I'm so sorry to take so long," Mrs. Adams said.

Belle turned and shook her head. "No worries. I was just looking."

The dark-skinned, rotund woman beamed, her eyes crinkling with joy. "What can I help you with, Belle? It is Belle, correct?"

"Yes, ma'am. I need a hobby."

"Okay." Her eyes widened with expectancy.

"Uh...I was thinking about knitting or crocheting, but I don't know the difference between the two." *Please tell me those are real things.*

"The basic difference is knitting uses two needles and crocheting uses a single hook." Mrs. Adams picked up a kit for knitting and one for crocheting. "You can see the needles and hook here."

"Which one is easier?"

"Oh honey, I wish I could tell you that. Every crocheter that walks in the door thinks it's easier to crochet than knit. Of course, the opposite could be said when a knitter walks in. Every now and then I get them smarty-pants that do both."

Belle chuckled. "Well, using one hook seems better than two." Especially since her wrist still aggravated her at times. She wouldn't fumble with just one hook.

"I'm sure the crocheters would agree. Besides, knitting produces a lighter material than crocheting. Considering the frigid wind out there, you might want to learn how to crochet."

"Sold."

"All right, let's get you all set. Any idea what you want to make?"

She shrugged. "A scarf?"

"I can help you with that." Mrs. Adams picked and plucked material after explaining them all.

Belle's head swam, but her insides were giddy with excitement. If she could dive in headfirst, maybe tedium would remain at bay and horrid memories would leave her in peace.

Once they made it to the cash register, Mrs. Adams met her gaze. "Can I help you find anything else?"

"No, ma'am. We'll see how this goes."

"Just have fun and it'll be easy peasy."

Belle thanked her and headed outside. She stopped, as the bright sunshine momentarily blinded her. Once her eyes adjusted, she noticed the red barn. Her stomach made a noise, hinting at her next stop. The Pit did have good food and she *did* skip breakfast. A glance at her watch told her breakfast could still be served if they were open.

She crossed the street, thankful the town didn't have a lot of traffic. The differences from her hometown stunned her at times. Maple Run seemed to have a more laid-back feel to it. Although the people in Charlotte were friendly, they had more speed to their movement as opposed to the people here. She hadn't yet decided which she preferred. Of course, Charlotte had more of an edge. She'd never been bored there.

*And you were never happy either.*

Life was always full of tradeoffs. What was one supposed to do with one's history and present living? It presented a quandary she just didn't know how to merge. Did she even want to? Her brow wrinkled as she opened the door to The Pit.

"Good morning, welcome back! I'm Nikki."

"Hi, Belle." She shook Nikki's offered hand.

"Are you joining anyone?"

"No. Just breakfast for one."

"No problem. Bar or table?"

"Bar, please." Then she wouldn't look like a loser sitting by herself.

Nikki placed a menu on the countertop in front of a vacant barstool. "Hey, Belle. I know you're new in town and may not know anyone. I was wondering if you'd like to join some of us ladies for a girls' night out."

"Uh..." Surprise floored her. She hadn't had female friends since high school, and even then, only one had been willing to reciprocate the friendship.

*Wonder where Jasmine is now?*

"You don't have to," Nikki continued.

Belle blinked, returning to the conversation.

"I just thought you might want to meet some people. Sorry if I put you on the spot. I have a tendency to talk a lot—without thinking—like now." Nikki's cheeks turned bright red.

Seeing the sincerity on her face pulled words from her mouth. "Thank you. I appreciate the invitation. When is the get-together?" *Is that what you called it?*

"It's next Friday at Nina's house. She's not here right now; otherwise, I'd introduce you. Delaney will be there. Have you met her?"

"She's a server, right?"

"Server and part owner."

*Wow. Why would an owner serve food? Were they that hard up, or was she that hands on?*

"This is a family restaurant, so the family works it. No standoffish people here." Nikki beamed.

"That explains the good food and atmosphere."

"So, will you come?"

"Yes." Her insides winced in fear. What would she say? Do?

*Anything you want, Belle. Be free.*

"Great!" Nikki clasped her hands together. "I'll give you my number. That way I can give you all the particulars later." She wrote on a notepad, tearing out the page. "Enjoy your breakfast."

"Thank you." She stared down at the paper, pleased that she might have finally made a friend. Maybe one who would help her discover who she could be.

"Fancy meeting you here."

Her body froze at the sound of Micah's voice.

*This town is way too small.*

Micah couldn't believe Belle chose to eat at The Pit. He figured she had a full social calendar. Her type usually did. A twinge of unease hit him in the gut. Was he being too judgmental? Hadn't she proven she was different? From the way she handled the patients and their concerns to the night she bought that TV, she'd proven there was more to her than a pretty face.

So why couldn't he let his preconceptions go?

*Fear.*

The answer came fast and swift and not one he wanted to examine.

"How are you, Mr. Campbell?" Belle's voice held a smidgen of warmth, but it hid under the layer of formality.

"All right. I'll be more so if you could drop the mister."

"Just Campbell?"

"Or Soup."

Her nose wrinkled, making her look closer to a teen than an adult and beyond cute. *Oh, boy.*

"I was in the Army. I don't know how to act when someone adds a mister or calls me by my first name."

Interest flared in her eyes. "What did you do?"

"Flight nurse." He sat down next to her. "Rode helicopters to pick up injured soldiers and triaged them, until we made it back to the hospital."

"Were you ever in danger?" She turned in her barstool, looking at him with her big brown eyes.

Eyes that tugged at him. He cleared his throat. "I might have been."

A shudder shook her frame. "Wow," she whispered. "That's very brave of you."

*She thought he was brave?* He sat there stunned. This was the longest conversation they had since she started work. "I'm not so sure. We're trained to do what we do. And I did it," he shrugged.

"A job you volunteered for."

"No different than going to work to be a nurse."

Belle stared at her hands and shrugged.

What was she thinking? A lot of people gave nurses and other medical staff grief. They wanted them to be God and heal them at the drop of a hat. Unfortunately, only One had the power to do so. Still, she handled everyone who walked through their office with care and compassion.

"You don't think nursing is an admirable job?" he asked.

"I didn't go in for the admiration."

"Then why did you?"

"The science." Her eyes twinkled. "I can't help it. I just love to see how the body works."

"You're a science nerd?"

She nodded. "Shocking, huh?"

*Definitely.* But he shook his head in disagreement. "Is it just the biology field or all science?"

Before she could answer, Shaunice came over and took their orders. Micah repeated the question once she left.

"All of it." She intertwined her fingers. Now what? What could she say to clear the dead silence taking over?

Micah met her gaze, a look of patience on his face. If he kept staring at her like that, she'd never survive the wait for their meals.

"Want to hear a joke?"

"Sure."

*Thank goodness.* She cleared her throat. "What do you do with a sick chemist?"

He raised an eyebrow. "I don't know. What?"

"If you can't helium, and you can't curium, then you might as well barium." She clutched her side laughing.

"That's awful," he groaned. Micah watched as she continued to snicker as if it were an award-winning joke.

Belle snorted, then slapped a hand over her mouth.

Laughter erupted from both of them.

"Oh...my...goodness," Belle gasped. "I love that joke."

"You know it's really terrible, right?"

"No way. It's cute. If you're lucky, I'll tell you more."

And she did until Shaunice placed their plates in front of them, shaking her head as she walked away. They had probably looked ridiculous laughing. Belle turned away and bowed her head over her food, whispering a prayer.

A shockwave washed over him. *She's a Christian.* And one that didn't mind praying in the middle of a restaurant. A spark of attraction lit inside him.

*No, God. I do not want to be attracted to her. Don't you remember what happened with Denise?* He closed his eyes, trying to repress the memories. "I don't remember you praying last time."

*You didn't either.* He winced inwardly as she widened her eyes.

"I usually don't in front of strangers."

He nodded, staring at his plate, and uttering a silent prayer. When his emotions were under control, he started mixing his eggs, grits, and bacon together. He reached for the salt and pepper shaker and paused when he saw Belle looking at his plate. "What?"

"You just mixed your food together." Her nose wrinkled up again.

She was beautiful. *Stop thinking like that. Focus, Soup.* "How else do you eat your eggs and grits?"

"Separately."

"Come again?"

"You eat grits with butter and sugar."

He grabbed his heart. "You've wounded me. Call Doc!"

Belle laughed, her cheekbones arching toward her eyes. "You'll need a doctor after you choke down that monstrosity on your plate."

"Belle, Belle, Belle. I can't believe you would dare put sugar in your grits. What kind of self-respecting Southern woman does so?"

"Everyone I know does. Didn't you know that's the new old-age question: salt or sugar."

"Sugar? Such a shame." He shook his head, then very deliberately, placed a heaping portion of his breakfast onto his spoon. Wiggling his eyebrows, he took a bite, making sure to grin in delight.

Belle made a gagging motion.

He held back his laughter, trying not to choke on his mouthful. "See, I told you, you were going to choke."

"Yeah, because some crazy woman was making faces while I ate." He offered a spoonful. "Try some."

"Ew, man germs."

His cheeks hurt from laughing so much.

"Besides, there's no sugar."

"How about this. I'll get you a fresh spoon and you try it. Then one day I'll try it your way."

Her expression dimmed. "No, thanks," she shook her head. "I'll stick to my yummy waffles."

They ate in silence. Well, relative silence. The Maple Pit always played music in the background. He glanced at Belle out of the corner of his eye. It was nice having a normal conversation with her without worrying if he would offend her. Except now, her likeability factor had shot up. That was a problem. A very, *big* problem.

His divorce from Denise had carved a pretty deep scar on his heart. He promised he'd never let another female have the power to do so again, but he couldn't ignore the attraction that had begun to spark around Belle. Then again, maybe he was worrying for nothing. Belle said she didn't want to date. Judging from the scar she tried to hide and her interaction with the slime ball, she wouldn't go out with him if it ever got to that point anyway.

So why did the thought bother him?

## 5

The damp cloth did nothing to cool her flaming cheeks. Belle closed her eyes in misery. Ever since she'd eaten breakfast with Micah, he'd made her pulse skitter into abnormal ranges. Today, he winked at her. *Winked!*

How could something so trivial set her face on fire? It's not like he flirted with her. No, it had simply been a tool to put the pediatric patient at ease. Yet, here she stood, hiding in the staff bathroom, to give herself a moment of reprieve. She begged her fluttering heart to calm as her eyes smarted with tears. She'd really hoped accepting Christ as her Savior would rid her of the desire to be noticed by another man. She didn't get it. Was she a glutton for punishment? Hadn't she learned her lesson?

She had visible scars to remind her of what happened when you went your own way. Even had nightmares that sent her stomach dry-heaving in the middle of the night. Why, oh why, did men still affect her? And Micah of all people.

*Why, Lord?*

Sure, he was the epitome of tall, dark, and handsome. No man should look that good bald. Worse, his humility and kindness were genuine. It would have been so much better if he had been arrogant and *knew* he looked good. But, no, the guy had to be one of the sweetest men she had ever met.

The way he interacted with patients, especially the kids, almost melted her heart. *Almost.* She was determined not to fall for his charm. Her cardigans had become thicker and she went up a size in scrubs hoping to repel any unwanted attention.

*But you do want his attention.*

A tear slipped down her cheek. She did. The voice in her head proved true, because she wanted Micah's attention. And if that was the case, then accepting Christ as her Savior hadn't created a new self. She was still the same self-absorbed person of old.

*Please don't leave me where You found me, Lord. I want to change. I want to devote my life to You. Please take this attraction away.*

At least she wasn't attracted to Dr. K. Then again, old men had never sparked her interest.

Her sports watch beeped, signaling the end of the day. Thank goodness, she didn't have to be back until Monday. Another week down. She dried her face then opened the bathroom door. If her luck held out, Micah would be gone, and she wouldn't have to check her hormones around him.

Silence greeted her ears. She sighed with relief and headed for the lockers. The place had cleared out as silence greeted her. After grabbing her personal items, she headed for her car and drove home—to her own place. The first place she'd paid for. So what if the silence made her cringe. It was hers, outfitted with a TV and crocheting supplies.

Belle groaned.

Crocheting wasn't as exciting as she had hoped. It didn't block memories from surfacing, or drown out the noise from her TV. At first, she had been enthralled by the activity. Knowing she could create something from a ball of yarn made her feel accomplished. However, that quickly faded when the ache in her wrist had intensified. The allure left. What would she do with the scarves she had created? She couldn't wear more than one at a time.

A grin lit her face. Maybe she could bring them to the girls' night. Nikki told her there would be four other women coming. She had five scarves, so there was enough for everyone. Happy with the plan, she shed her scrubs and readied herself for the ladies' night out. Or in, considering it was at Nina Warrenton's home. Apparently, Nina was married to one of The Pit's chefs who was also an owner.

After changing into jeans and a cable-knit sweater, she threw a crocheted beanie on her head and wrapped a scarf around her neck. At least her new hobby had perks. Now, she could tolerate the frigid weather that had blown in from the Midwest.

Ten minutes later, she found herself in front of a gorgeous home. Layered stone steps led to a huge front porch that looked like it wrapped around all the way to the back. The cream-and-brown stone home shined bright thanks to the white lights outlining the place.

Before she knocked on the front door, Belle whispered a prayer. "Lord, please let this go okay. Help me to fit in and know what to say. Pretty please, help me make a friend or two. Amen. Here goes." She knocked on the door.

A petite female with a pixie cut opened the door. "Hi, you must be Belle. I'm Nina."

"Nice to meet you." She tried to smile through the fear.

"Come on in." Nina stepped aside, holding the door wide. "Are you allergic to dogs?"

"No," she responded slowly. "At least, I don't think so. I've never been around pets before."

"Well, Beast is gentle. He won't bother you unless you show him some love."

Belle followed her into the biggest kitchen she'd ever seen. Delaney and Nikki were seated at a table in the breakfast nook area. A handsome man closed the fridge. A thin goatee lined the area around his mouth and chin. He paused in front of Nina to drop a quick kiss on her lips.

"See you later, babe."

"Stay out of trouble."

He chuckled. "Likewise."

Nina laid a hand on his arm. "Wait a sec. Dwight, this is Belle. She's the nurse that works with Micah."

"Oh, hey." He shook her hand.

*Nothing.* No chills or sparks, despite his obvious good looks. Maybe God did answer prayer. "Nice to meet you."

"You too." He turned to Nina. "You need me to take Beast with me?"

"No, just the twins."

"Got it." He waved to them. "Have a nice night, ladies."

"Bye, D." Delaney called.

Nikki and Delaney walked toward her.

"I'm so glad you came." Nikki gave her a hug.

"Thanks for inviting me." *Ha!* A remembered lesson from her mother's admonishments. Despite her discomfort from the hug, she could still use her manners. Belle couldn't remember the last time she'd been around so many other ladies, and there were only three of them.

"No problem." Nikki grinned. "Belle, you remember Delaney? She's Dwight's twin sister. Nina is his wife and mama to his twins."

"Twins? I can't even imagine." She stared at Nina's bulging stomach. *And having another one.* "Are you having..." She trailed off. Wasn't there some rule you weren't supposed to ask a woman if she was pregnant?

"Just one this time."

"Congratulations."

A huge smile lit the petite woman's face. "Thanks. He's probably the last one. Four is enough."

*I'll say.* There was no way she could keep up with four children. "How old are your kids?"

"Kandi's almost 19. We adopted her at sixteen. The twins will be one in February. And the little one is due in three months." She patted her belly.

Belle turned to Delaney. "What about you? Do you have any children?"

"I have twin boys. They're ten going on twenty."

"More twins?"

"Family hazard," Delaney snorted.

"Are you and Luke going to have more kids once you get married?" Nikki asked.

"Oh, no. I'm too old for that."

"Thirty isn't old." *She* was thirty.

"Ah, Belle, you just made my day. I'm pushing forty."

Her mouth dropped open.

"I'm not far behind," Nina exclaimed.

"I'm thirty-three," Nikki said.

"I'm the youngest one here?" That never happened. The men Garrett had associated with, kept younger women around. It was part of their mid-life crisis or something. But the ten years' difference between her and Garrett hadn't bothered her. Just his personality. Her stomach clenched.

*No thoughts of Garrett tonight.*

"Guess so." Delaney leaned against the counter. "So, did I imagine sparks between you and Micah at The Pit the other day?"

"No!" Her response got lost amidst the laughter.

"Come on, Belle," Nikki said. "You guys looked pretty chummy at breakfast."

"I'm afraid I have some sort of plague where any able-bodied male would attract my interest."

"Like my husband?" Nina said, an eyebrow arched regally.

"Uh, no. Sorry, he doesn't do it for me." *Thank the good Lord.*

"Luke?" Delaney asked, with a secretive look on her face.

"No, sorry." She sighed. "Look, they're good-looking but they have nothing on..." She stopped, realizing where her thoughts were going.

41

The ladies doubled over with laughter, but she stood frozen, too stunned by the revelation to pay much attention. The skipping heartbeat, rapid pulse, flushed face...only happened when Micah was nearby. Neither Luke nor Dwight had elicited the reaction.

God had answered her prayers and opened Pandora's box in one fell swoop.

※

Micah opened his front door.

Dwight stood there holding boxes of soda. "I come bearing gifts," he deadpanned.

"Thanks, man. Come on in. Luke's already here." He headed for the kitchen.

"Cool. My boy Shorty will be over soon. He had a business matter come up."

"No problem."

"I would have been here sooner, but I had to drop the kids off at the babysitter's."

"Hello," squawked Noodle.

Dwight froze, staring at the birdcage. "You have a bird," he uttered in shock.

"African grey," Noodle responded.

"He doesn't like being called a bird." Micah stifled a laugh.

"And here I thought I won the award for coolest pet."

"Beast is impressive, but he can't talk." Luke smiled as he came to stand by them.

"Humph," Dwight snorted. "Nina would beg to differ."

"The lady's in love." Luke replied. "People in love do strange things."

"That's the truth," Micah mumbled.

He shook his head at the sappy look that crossed his friends' faces. Luke had come to Maple Run to make amends to Delaney.

He felt personally responsible for her late husband's death. In the process, they fell in love and were now engaged. "How did all my friends end up married men?"

"We're mature." Dwight said, with a shrug. "Comes with the territory."

"Nah, none of your stories are stereotypical." Micah headed for the kitchen to grab some food.

The guys followed.

"You answered an ad," Micah pointed at Dwight. "And Luke...well, he takes on the world's problems." He grabbed a bowl of chips and dip. "If I ever decide to marry again, I hope I fall in love the old-fashioned way."

"Like an office romance?" Dwight waggled his eyebrows.

The doorbell rang, bringing relief in its wake. He set the bowls down and went to answer it.

Shorty stood on his front porch. "Brought some wings."

"Awesome. Hopefully, you can save me from the married people." He rolled his eyes.

Shorty laughed. "Dwight hasn't been the same since he met Nina. I gotta admit though, they work."

Micah stopped in the hallway before his kitchen. "They do, but that doesn't mean the rest of the world will."

"True that," Shorty replied.

Gregory Smalls wasn't exactly short, but he wasn't tall either. His nickname had been a play on words and a nod to his height in comparison to the rest of his friends. At five ten, he still beat the average height for males, and remained shorter than the rest of them.

"Shorty's here." Micah announced, holding the platter of wings. "Shall we move to the basement?"

"Definitely," Luke replied. "I'll grab the chips and dip."

"I got the drinks," Dwight said.

"I got..." Shorty paused. "Need me to grab anything?"

"Bird cage. Noodles doesn't like to be alone."

Shorty looked at the cage skeptically. "How about I take my wings back and you grab Noodles." He stopped and looked at Micah. "You taking the whole Campbell's Soup thing a little far, aren't you?"

Dwight guffawed.

Luke grinned sheepishly. "I named him."

"Soldiers," Shorty said with a snort.

They all headed down to the basement. Micah's projection screen had already been set up, pointing toward the empty wall across from his sectional sofa. It was game time.

"Micah, my man," Shorty said. "I may have to trade in my flat screen for a projection."

"No kidding," Luke said.

"Watching football is a blast. Don't worry, I'll have a Super Bowl party." He smiled at his friends.

The guys threw a fist in the air at his proclamation. They'd probably make the Super Bowl watching entertaining with their humor, then again, they'd most likely be glued to the screen. With a click of a button, the projector came on and he turned it to the college football game.

During the commercial break, Dwight turned to him. "You know I didn't forget the conversation you avoided earlier."

"What's going on?" Shorty asked.

"Micah evaded the question of the relationship going on between him and Belle."

"The pretty nurse?" Shorty asked.

Micah's gut tightened. He thought Shorty was interested in Nikki. Hadn't he implied as much? Micah asked him.

"Nah, Nikki and I are just friends." Shorty turned his attention back to the screen.

Dwight snorted. "Friends, huh?"

Shorty glared at his best friend.

"Look, I won't say that all men need to marry." Dwight crossed his leg. "However, it does say in the Bible, 'He who finds a wife finds a good thing.'"

"Been there, done that, got the divorce certificate." One strike was enough to keep him single.

"Yeah, but Denise was a piece of work," Luke said.

"Denise is the ex?" Dwight asked, looking between him and Luke.

"Yes," Micah sighed. "She cheated while I was deployed. With my cousin. Now they're living happily ever after, so I avoid family gatherings for that reason."

"That's tough, Soup, but you can't let that keep you from God's blessings. Who knows, maybe Belle is such a blessing," Luke said in his Texas drawl.

Silence descended as the game came back on.

He wanted to argue with his friends but stopped himself, contemplating Luke's words. His request for a second-chance love had been forgotten as he'd worked toward getting his physician assistant license. Now that he'd been successful, he had been intent on enjoying life. Could Belle be part of God's plan for his life?

During the next commercial break, Shorty started the conversation again. "That's a tough spot to be in. If you have any baggage from that relationship, don't do it. Better to let her go and find someone else who can love her the way she needs. Even if she doesn't want your love."

Micah raised an eyebrow. Sounded like Shorty had his own relationship drama.

"Well, since everyone else chimed in, I'll throw in my two cents." Dwight said. "Go to God. Ask Him if you should pursue a relationship with Belle. And don't tell me you're not interested. Sparks lit up The Pit when you two were in there."

Laughter didn't necessarily equate with sparks. But that was the lie he'd told himself all week. "Okay, so she's gorgeous. But we work together. That's never a good thing."

"Isn't that the normal way to fall in love? At a place you both frequent?" Luke asked.

The question hung in the air as the game came back on and the guys' focus turned back to the action. When God said no to a new relationship, Micah became intent on avoiding past mistakes, or women who were like Denise. Could it be God was trying to get his attention? Could Belle be more than a coworker? It was something he would have to think about. For now, he'd enjoy the down time, the game, and leave relationship contemplation for another day.

## 6

Christmas music greeted her ears as Belle walked into Mable's Crafting Corner. The music reminded her of the movie, *Home Alone.*

Mrs. Adams looked up from behind the cash register. "Good morning, Belle."

"Morning, Mrs. Adams."

"You can call me Ms. Mable, Belle."

She loved how the older generation went by the formalities. "Thank you."

"You need some yarn or other supplies?" Ms. Mable came around the counter, hands clasped together.

"Actually," she bit her lip. "I don't think crocheting is for me." She winced. *Did her words sound callous?*

"Don't go looking all timid on me, Belle. Nothing wrong with stating your mind from time to time. Do you need something a little more challenging?"

"Um, I'm not sure." Should she bring up the pain in her wrist?

"Let me think, let me think," Ms. Mable muttered, tapping the edge of her chin with her forefinger.

The woman's eyes scanned her store as if searching for the

right craft that would put an end to Belle's endless boredom. At least, that's what she hoped Ms. Mable was searching for.

"Ah-ha!" The older woman charged across the store, intent on her mission.

Belle followed more sedately. As they drew closer, she stopped short. Beads, charms, and everything needed to make jewelry glistened before her. Her breath caught at the gorgeous display. The colors and femininity of it all called to her. Her hand reached out, taking hold of a beautiful black bead, which swirled with an array of colors.

"I thought you might like this section. You have a natural beauty that shines and also allows for jewelry to make a perfect complement. Jewelry making can be a challenge. There are so many different ways to create bracelets, earrings, and necklaces. You name it, I have it."

"I can't," she whispered. Her heart shattered into million pieces. She knew vanity was her stumbling block and pretty jewels would just make it worse.

"Of course, you can. Granted, it's more expensive than crocheting, so your pocket book will take a hit. But I guarantee you'll have fun, Belle dear."

She shook her head. Images of glitz and glamour swirled in her mind. When God pulled her out of the gutter, Belle promised she'd never draw attention to herself. Never put herself in the situation to attract attention that wasn't hers to begin with. She'd purged herself of dresses, makeup, and all her precious jewelry. A person like her didn't deserve those things anyway.

"Ms. Mable, perhaps you can recommend another hobby." She put the beads back on the rack, folding her arms around her waist.

"Is it the cost of it all?" Ms. Mable asked cautiously.

"No, ma'am. I have no purpose for jewelry."

"Course I never seen you wear any, but you look like a girl who admires pretty things."

*Too often.* And where had it gotten her? Physical and emotional scars laced her being because she'd been thinking of materialistic wealth when she chose a mate. "Pretty things can become an idol."

"That they can." A look of curiosity filled the woman's eyes. "If you keep your eyes on the good Lord, it won't."

No, she couldn't risk it. "Thanks anyway, Ms. Mable. I guess I'll just take some more yarn."

"If you're sure..."

Belle wasn't, but it was what it was. Moving forward remained her purpose. She couldn't let the materialistic life of the past call to her. "I'm sure."

After making her purchase, she left. The Pit called to her, begging for her to stop by, but she couldn't do it. Couldn't risk that she'd run into Micah and wonder. Wonder what it would be like to flirt and enter into a relationship. She was too damaged. Too dirty from past sins.

*Why did You pull me out of the gutter, Lord? Wouldn't it have been better to leave me there?*

The heaviness of depression pushed down upon her. Tears distorted her vision. It was stupid to think that she could become something new. Something not filled with shame and guilt. Something worthy of love and affection.

*You do love me, right, Lord?*

*"Yea, I have loved thee with an everlasting love."*

Peace filled her heart. She remembered the verse from last week's devotional reading. God's love was everlasting. If He was the only one who could love her, that would be enough.

She'd make it enough.

Determination fueled her steps toward her hatchback. Time to go home and watch TV and crochet. It had become her new normal. She needed to embrace that rather than bemoan the fact. Surely, it would remind her of what God brought her out of. She opened her car door.

"Belle!"

Her eyes closed in defeat. Why was that man everywhere?

49

Reluctantly, she turned and saw Micah jogging toward her. He must have been going to The Pit or just leaving it.

"Hey, thanks for waiting up." He smiled at her as if it was okay that he inserted himself into her life.

"Did you need something?" She hoped her back-off sign could be seen or at least heard.

Judging by the arch of his one annoying eyebrow, the message had been received. *Drat!* Why did he look so good arching that one brow?

"I wanted to ask if you would join me for breakfast." He gestured toward The Pit.

"I don't think so. I'm headed home." *To craft, like an old lady.* What had her life come to?

"On a Saturday? You're not going to go out?"

"I went out last night. Besides," She threw her hand up in the air. "Please tell me what there is to do in this town."

"Are you hangry? Because you seem to have an attitude this morning. Food in your belly will help that real quick." The corner of his mouth lifted as if to signal he was joking.

"You don't know me, so don't presume you know what will 'fix' me." Her anger rose quickly, blocking everything out, including the fact she used air quotes. If she'd been in her right mind, she'd be aghast by the cliché action.

"Belle, I don't know what's bothering you, but you can talk to me."

His soft tone immobilized her. Tears welled up and spilled over before she could tame them. *Lord, stop these tears! I can't cry in front of him.* She swiped at them, but it was no use. They fell faster than her fingers could wipe them away.

She whirled around, hoping he would take the hint and leave.

"Belle, talk to me."

A warm hand touched her shoulder softly.

"Go away, Campbell."

"Oh, *now* you call me Campbell."

The warmth of his touch increased as he moved closer. "It doesn't work."

"What?" She croaked.

"Bottling your emotions. They'll erupt sooner or later. I promise I'm a good listener."

"I can't go in there looking like this." Her eyes always puffed up with redness when she cried. It didn't matter if one tear shed or a hundred. Her eyes took on the appearance of Rocky after the last round.

He turned her around, his hands on both shoulders now. "If you're nice to me, I could be persuaded to cook you breakfast."

His words couldn't have been more shocking than a bucket of ice water. "Somehow, I thought you were different."

She wrenched free and got in her car, driving away without a backward glance.

꒰ꔛ꒱

If they had lived in the desert, a trail of dust would have been left behind by Belle's tiny car. It was bad enough seeing the brake lights as she turned down the road.

Guilt swallowed Micah whole. He'd made her feel cheap. No words needed to be spoken for that message to come across loud and clear. As soon as the words left his mouth, he wanted to recall them, remembering that awful night when she'd bought the TV.

How could he explain to her that he didn't mean it that way? Judging by the speed in which she'd left, she wouldn't be seeking him out any time soon.

A groan slipped free. "I'm an idiot, Lord."

"Don't be too hard on yourself, Campbell." Ms. Mable said, interrupting his pity party. "That girl's got a heavy dose of heartache she's working through."

He turned toward the Crafting Corner. Of course, someone would witness his misery. "And I just added to it."

"Then you better make it right."

He slid his hands into his jacket pockets. "I don't know how."

"Here," she handed him a gift bag. "Take this to her. Tell her I said it's a gift."

"Giving her your gift isn't going to help me, Ms. Mable."

"No, but it'll give you the opening you need."

With that, she hurried back into the store, the jingle of the bell tinkling as it closed shut.

Was he really supposed to show up at her house with a gift from Ms. Mable? He'd be lucky if she didn't call the police for stalking or something.

*Go.*

The word echoed in his heart. He winced, running a hand over his chin. *Lord, I'm not sure if that's You, but that seems like a really bad idea.*

*Go.*

The urge to pout and stomp his foot rose strongly within him, but the urge to obey grew even stronger. He could only pray that the voice was really of God and not some sick, twisted prank of his mind.

Crossing the street, he headed for The Pit, where his SUV sat parked. He paused in front of the doorway. Should he grab breakfast? It could be a peace offering.

*Or presumptuous.*

Unease niggled in his belly. Okay, he'd skip breakfast. No need to make it worse by showing up to her place uninvited with breakfast. He winced. Why had the thought even entered his mind? *Wise up, Campbell.*

It took no time for him to pull up to Belle's place, so Micah sat there staring at the steering wheel. The urge to go in had become stronger, but so had the fear. "Lord, please don't let me make things worse. Please guard my lips and only let sincerity and wisdom come out. *Please.*"

With a whispered "Amen," he got out of the vehicle and headed up the walkway. Despite his slow and steady pace, he made it to her second-floor apartment sooner than his nerves were ready for. The door knocker stared at him, the gold gleaming against the white door.

He knocked before he could change his mind. Footfalls reached his ear before the sound of the door unlocking. Anxiety gripped him, urging his heartbeats closer together.

A look of shock distorted Belle's pretty features. "*What* are you doing here?" She stepped on the stair landing, shutting her door behind her.

"I came to apologize." He rushed out, backing up to give her ample room. "I didn't mean for my words to have that kind of meaning. I only meant it in a friendly, non-threatening, non-sexual manner." He paused, realizing he'd begun to ramble.

"Then what *did* you mean?"

"Just that if you asked, I probably would have made breakfast. That's it." He spread his hands out, then realized he had Ms. Mable's gift. "Oh, this is from Ms. Mable. She asked me to bring it by."

"Thank you."

He nodded, hoping the grudging tone meant he was on the road to forgiveness. "I'm sorry for being careless in my words. I know you've been through a lot. I just want to be a friend." *I think.*

A hint of wariness entered her eyes. "I don't know what you mean."

Did he voice his thoughts or leave? He sighed. "I think you've been hurt before. I just want you to know not all men are like that."

She snorted.

"See? Give me a chance to prove a man can be a good friend, without wanting something in return." *Oh, Lord, please don't let me make a liar out of myself.*

"Micah, you don't owe me any explanations. There's nothing for you to prove."

"Yes, there is. Please." He put his hands together in benediction. The feeling deep down in his soul told him Belle needed a friend. A true one. One who would put her needs above their own.

She bit her lip. "What does that entail? You proving men can be friends?"

"How does weekly breakfast at The Pit sound? We could meet every Saturday."

Silence greeted his ears.

"I'm not sure."

*Fair enough.* "What about a friend to sit by in church?"

Indecision entered her eyes, darkening them to pools of milk chocolate. Gorgeous eyes. *No, friendly eyes.*

"I can handle that."

"Hanging out outside of work?"

Her head shook so fast, her hair almost whipped into her eyes.

"No worries. We'll work up to that." Looked like he'd need all the skills in patience he could muster.

Something told him Belle Peterson would require every last drop he could manage. *Lord, please give me a divine gift of patience. Please, help me show her I can be a friend.*

"Would you like to go to breakfast, friend?" He waited for what seemed like forever before she responded.

"Not today, Campbell."

His heart dipped. *She's not ready.* He nodded his head. "Okay, then I'll see you at church tomorrow?"

She gave a short nod of her head and then turned and went inside. Micah stood on the threshold, staring at the closed door. As much as he wanted to deny it, Belle spiked his attraction meter. Something no woman had managed to do in years. Okay, so there had been other women, but none of them had made him want to act on the interest. How could he show her he could be a friend when one look from her sent his pulse racing?

It would take the strength of the Lord and a whole lot of prayer to behave himself. *You'll help me, Lord, right?*

Peace soothed his soul as he realized this is what the Lord had been preparing him for. It couldn't be a coincidence that patience had been his request for the last couple of months. God knew Belle would enter his life. And only God knew what would happen.

He lifted his hand in farewell, although she couldn't see him, and headed down her stairs. Tomorrow would provide a fresh start and he needed to be ready to put her needs above his own. If he wanted to show her he had the mental fortitude and endurance to handle whatever she threw at him, he'd need to be prayed up and studied up.

## 7

Church. It wasn't something in which Belle had vast experience. Okay, *one* previous experience. She hadn't stepped foot in one until the kindness of a stranger had her seeking God. Part of her felt she should tell Micah. Would he expect her to know the words to the songs? Sing and shout? Did they even do that or was that something in the movies?

Belle shook her head as her vehicle navigated through the church parking lot. Surely, there would be an empty spot somewhere. Then again, the lot ran on the small side. Not that the patrons of Maple Run needed a big one, not like the lots she'd passed time and again in Charlotte.

"Lord," she whispered. "Why do I keep thinking about that place? I can't go backwards. Help me keep my eyes on the prize."

After placing the car in park, she swung her car door open.

"Good morning, Belle." Micah smiled, shading his eyes against the blinding sun.

"Morning."

Such an anomaly. How the sun could shine so brightly in frigid temperatures was beyond her. She expected gray and dreary skies. Not sunshine and blue so bright it begged one to reach out and touch it. The wind whipped in the air, going right through her jacket and into her drab pantsuit. Today the added winter accessories proved futile.

"Let's go inside," Micah grumbled.

She nodded, moving her head just enough to acknowledge his statement and not so much to jolt it from the scarf wrapped around her neck. North Carolina had been experiencing more cold temperatures, but nothing prepared her for the frigid Virginia wind. It felt like the cold touch of death had wrapped its way around her. How did people enjoy this season?

Spring was the only season to make her heart beat with joy. She held onto the thought as she forged through the wind and into the open foyer. Flowers would be coming after this. Right? Belle sighed in relief as warmth greeted her like a long-lost family member in the church foyer. She unraveled her scarf. "Goodness, it's cold out."

"No kidding." Micah took his gloves off, placing them in his coat pockets. "I'm glad you still came out. The Pastor is a great teacher and speaker of the Word. I'm sure you'll learn a lot."

The hopeful expression on his face made her stomach twist in fear. "Um, Micah, there's something I need to say."

"Sure, what's up?" He slid his hands into his slacks.

"I've only been to church once." *In a hospital chapel.* "I'm a Christian," she rushed out. "Just newly saved."

"Congratulations!" His goatee seemed to stretch to accommodate the bright white grin showcased against his ebony skin. "Then you'll really love him. He doesn't talk in a way that will confuse you."

"Okay."

Stunned was the only word she could think of, and the only reason 'okay' made it past her lips. She figured he would look at her with horror or past judgement. Instead, the grin that lit his face caused her pulse to speed up.

There was no doubt she was alive and kicking this morning.

Micah led the way down the Berber carpeted aisle. Mahogany pews filled the white chapel of Maple Run Community Church. Faces she recognized from Dr. Kerrington's practice smiled at her. She even recognized some from The Maple Pit. The sense of community and fellowship overwhelmed her. Maybe it wouldn't be so bad after all.

It almost seemed like they accepted her, warts and all.

*Oh, but if they only knew.*

She blinked, trying to push the voice away. It seemed to rear its ugly head at the most inopportune times. Why was it allowed in church? Was nothing sacred?

"I'm loved," she whispered.

"What's that?" Micah looked at her as he settled into the pew.

"Oh, nothing. Just thinking how lovely this church is." She pointed to the stained glass in the cross-shaped cutout behind the pulpit. "That's gorgeous."

It reminded her of the baubles Ms. Mable had sent with Micah. The jewelry kit had been a complete surprise *and* an unwelcomed one. Ms. Mable had even included a note.

*To create beauty is a gift from above.*
*"Every good gift and every perfect gift is from above..." James 1:17 KJV*
*Don't waste God's gift.*
*Mable Adams*

"Dwight said they had a fundraiser to get one put in," Micah said, pulling her to the present. "Apparently, they used to have a cross in the back. I think the stained glass is more breathtaking, don't you?"

"Definitely." She offered an uneasy smile.

Was there enough space between them? He'd placed his Bible between them, but it didn't seem like a big enough gap. What were the rules of proper church-like behavior? Sometimes, she wished God had been introduced to her sooner. Other times, she wished He hadn't bothered. Who was she to be absolved of a sin so great it left permanent scars?

"That's the pastor," Micah whispered, leaning close.

A man in a blue-checkered, button-up shirt, and gray slacks stood behind the podium. Hmm, she thought he'd wear a suit. The ones on TV usually did.

"Let us stand." The pastor paused as everyone stood. "I'll open in prayer."

Again, surprise filled her. She expected the prayer to be filled with words she didn't understand. Her mother had always taught her that Christians thought they were smarter than everyone and some of the ones she'd seen on TV made no sense to her. Yet, the direct and easy manner in which the pastor spoke, put her at ease. Perhaps she could follow along and actually learn something today. The good Lord knew she struggled reading her King James Bible.

Still, she wouldn't give up trying. It had been a gift from a dear friend. Belle would feel like a failure if she couldn't read the whole thing. Isn't that what one did?

A chorus of "Amens" filled the air, startling her from her reverie. Heat flushed her cheeks as she realized her mind had wandered through half of the prayer. Five minutes in church and she was already messing up.

Sweet music floated in the air, swirling around her, beckoning her to lift her arms and cast her worries aside. Belle swayed back and forth as one of the women on stage began singing. Her voice evoked the likeness of an angel, and Belle thanked God for the gift of salvation. Tears sprang to her eyes.

Yes, she was unworthy. Yes, she'd committed a sin and had done horrible things in her past. But this...this was why she accepted Jesus as her Savior. The sense of rightness and completion that came when one became His echoed in her heart as the words touched her. She'd never heard the song before, but the words rang true.

The song came to a close and another one immediately started. It had a more upbeat tempo but was no less powerful. Her earlier fears faded away. It seemed ridiculous that she'd been afraid of going to church. Yet somehow, she thought her sins would be as evident as a scarlet letter, proving she had no place in the church, nor the community.

The song ushered in praise and a sense of belonging. Her worries were apparently unfounded. What else could she be wrong about?

※

Micah exhaled slowly as the pastor ended his sermon. It had been just what he needed. Nothing compared to hearing a much-needed message after a rough week. Sure, work had gone smoothly, but this thing with Belle...well, that had been the main focus of his prayers.

He added a prayer of thanks to the Lord for the bloom he saw in her. She seemed to have blossomed throughout the service. The shadows that haunted her eyes faded away with each song of worship. By the last one, she had been clapping and tapping her feet to the music. She even smiled at him occasionally.

The church service had changed her and, it had done the same for him. When he vowed to be a good friend to her, no strings attached, he'd been perfectly aware that it was a somewhat foolish desire. Could a man really be friends with a woman? He'd always thought so, but now he had to admit, his feelings were already skirting the line past friendly. Everything about her tugged at him, intrigued him, and consumed his thoughts night and day.

When he was around her, he wanted to protect her and show her how life could be. Those feelings were more in the attracted camp versus I-can-be-a-good-friend-with-no-complications side. He shook his head at his absurdity. *Lord, please help me push this attraction to the back burner. I know in my heart that she needs healing.*

*It's screaming from her soul, Lord. A romantic relationship will only complicate matters. Please help me to keep my promise. May I be the friend she needs.*

When the service ended, and Micah stood with the rest of the congregation, shaking hands with his church family. Belle laid a hand on his arm. "I see the girls. I'm going to go say hi. I just wanted to thank you again for inviting me."

"No problem. We'll do this again next Sunday." He bit back the disappointment as she looked toward them, but he couldn't begrudge her desire for female friends. He forced a smile to his face. "Sounds great. See you at work."

With a wave, she left the pew and headed toward Nikki and Delaney.

After greeting a few other people, he decided to leave. There would be no Bible study today and eventually, football would be on TV. He might as well go home and be comfortable. Funny how the familiar walls of his home all of a sudden seemed restrictive.

"Soup."

He turned at the sound of his name. Luke stood in the aisle, gesturing for him to come near. Nina, Dwight, Delaney, Nikki, and Belle all stood around him.

"What's up?"

"We're hungry." Luke said with no preamble. "Dee's mom offered to feed us."

"Where is Mrs. Williams?" He looked around but didn't see the formidable woman.

"She went to get the boys, so we could see who's coming over," Delaney said. She stood, her arm hooked around Luke, standing as close as possible but still maintaining propriety.

He was happy his friend found someone to be with. Luke deserved it and from what he knew about Delaney, she as well.

"You coming?" Dwight asked.

"Yes." *Of course!* Another opportunity to be around Belle? He'd take it. *Just go slow, Campbell. No need to be manic in your eagerness.*

"Great. We can head there now. Mama said there's no need to bring anything," Dwight said with a clap of his hands.

Micah followed the line of cars to the Williamses' family home. Thankfully, they had a long driveway to accommodate the influx of cars. He exited his car after he parked behind Belle's.

"You're going to enjoy hanging out with everyone," he said.

She turned, and a look of fear flashed in her eyes. His strides carried him over in seconds. "What's wrong?"

"I don't usually hang out in a crowd."

"Introvert?"

"No, I just don't know how to handle questions."

"Don't worry. They're a great group of people. Mrs. Williams can be a bit much from time to time, but at least she'll feed you."

Belle laughed.

"There you go. All better?"

"Yes, thank you."

"Anytime, friend."

He motioned for her to go forward, despite the fact that he wanted to offer his arm. Seeing her laugh and smile did him in. It was like she gave him a glimpse of who she could be if the chains constraining her were broken. He wondered how much abuse she had suffered to make her afraid of living life. Was her father the first person to earn her mistrust? A boyfriend?

Come to think of it, she never mentioned family or anyone else. Was she alone? Surely, there was someone in her past who cared about her. *Right, Lord?*

A niggling feeling squirmed in his gut. His parents loved him and checked on him regularly. Of course, he did the same. They were getting up there in age but refused to let it slow them down. His father cut his own lawn every Saturday to prove his independence—and had the best-looking house on their street in Annapolis.

Micah rubbed his chin as he followed the crew into the house. Maybe a road trip was necessary. It'd been a while since he took the time to visit his parents. Since he moved from Bethesda to Maple Run, it seemed like he saw them less and less.

A cacophony of noise greeted his ears as he neared the living room. Philip and Preston, Delaney's twin boys, were sword-fighting with string cheese. Nina's twins, Gabe and Abby, were trying to stand on their chubby legs, clapping with glee as they watched their older cousins.

Dwight and Mrs. Williams cooked in the kitchen, making magic happen. Micah inhaled the scents beginning to drift forward.

"Is it always like this?" Belle asked, her eyes wide with speculation.

"I don't usually come over when everyone is home. Just for the occasional guys' night."

"Yeah, it was much quieter for girls' night."

Philip shouted with joy as Preston lay on the carpet, tongue hanging out. "I foiled him." Philip threw a fist pump in the air.

"Philip, please be careful." Delaney said. "Your little cousins are close by."

"I know, Mama." He picked up Abby. "Abby likes sword-fighting, don't you?"

Her giggle filled the air.

"Aww," Belle whispered. "She's so adorable. All that curly hair."

"I'm just praying it won't be super long," Nina said, coming to stand by them. "Can you see me braiding hair?"

"Sure, why not," Belle said with a shrug. "It's a skill that can be learned."

"No way. I missed that boat. If Kandi were here, she'd be able to do it."

"How's she enjoying art school?" He thought it was so amazing that they adopted a teenager from foster care. Most people didn't do that, and it seemed to be even less prevalent in the African-American community.

"She loves it. I miss her. I feel the urge to walk through an art museum just to feel closer to her."

"I love art," Belle said with a small smile.

"Really?" Micah turned to Belle. She seemed to hide behind neutral colors. He would have never guessed that.

"There's something about putting all of your emotions out there for the world to see. Will they accept you or shun you?" She gave a delicate shudder. "I couldn't be an artist, but I appreciate them."

And the dichotomy continued. *Who is this woman, Lord?* "You're an interesting person to know, Belle Peterson."

"Um…thanks?"

## 8

Never had she been a part of something so chaotic...and utterly amazing. Platters were passed around as hands grabbed, served, and continued the forward movement of food. Christmas music played through the home entertainment system, the words of "Deck the Halls" adding to the volume of noise. Apparently, Dwight had installed the surround-sound system. It seemed he took care of the repairs at the Williams home that Delaney, her twins, and her mother shared.

Belle turned to Delaney. "Where will you live after you get married?"

"Here."

"With your mother?" Her forehead wrinkled up. "Luke's going to allow that?"

"It was his idea."

She resisted the urge to pick at the anomaly of Delaney's fiancé. What guy *wanted* to live with his mother-in-law? It made no sense. "Is it...finances?"

Delaney paused mid-bite, then set her fork down. "No, actually. She told me she wanted us to move in. Offered to move out and everything, which was a surprise," Delaney leaned close, her voice low. "I was afraid to bring it up to Luke. I wasn't sure how he'd react, but he was okay with the idea of her staying. I can't just kick my mother out, so he's been renovating the basement into a mother-in-law suite. He just finished the bathroom. I can show you after lunch, it's amazing. She's happy. The boys are happy. I'm happy."

Delaney picked up her fork and resumed eating.

Belle stared at her plate, food arranged so that nothing touched. What would it have been like to have her mother living with her or nearby? Garrett wouldn't have stood for it. Then again, her relationship with her mother had been strained for years now. The one time she tried to contact her mother, she'd ignored her pleas and marked her as irresponsible and spoiled.

Look where that got her. A hospital bill and a desire for a new life. Her relationship with the Lord was the only silver lining. Maybe one day, she'd bridge the gap with her mother. After all, it'd been years since Belle had seen or talked to her. Even when she lay in the hospital begging for death, her mother never showed.

No one did except Cara.

Micah nudged her with his arm. "You okay?"

*No.* "Food's good," she said instead. No need to bare her soul. It would only lead to more questions. Ones she had no intention of answering.

"So, Belle," Mrs. Williams said. "How do you like working at Dr. Kerrington's office?"

The older woman's brown skin glowed with a gracefulness Belle hoped she'd have in a few decades. Mrs. Williams dark hair fell in soft waves to her shoulder, but a pinched look marred her features.

Belle swallowed her food, fighting for composure. "I like it. He's great to work for. Plus, the rest of the staff makes the day enjoyable." Her face heated up under the scrutiny.

It was like being called on for school. Belle never wanted the other kids to know she knew the answers. Her mother taught her at a young age that beauty outweighed smarts. Only now, she used smarts instead of beauty. After what had happened, she'd be insane to think that beauty was the better choice.

"Mimi is a wonderful lady." Mrs. Williams remarked. "She runs a lot of the potlucks at church."

"Oh, I didn't see her."

"She works in the nursery," Nina said. "The kids love her."

"Mimi's great with the kids at the practice." She smiled at Nina, thankful for the other woman's friendship.

"Are you?" Mrs. Williams asked.

"I beg your pardon?" The staccato tone of Mrs. Williams unnerved her. Was the woman short-tempered or simply nosy? Belle took a bite of her food, contemplating the personality of the matriarch.

"Are you good with kids? You know it's an important part of marriage."

Part of her mashed potatoes flew from her mouth and across the table, the rest dribbling down her face. Delaney snickered next to her. Nina rolled her eyes, yet it didn't seem to be directed toward her. Micah handed her a napkin.

"Thank you," she mumbled. She wiped her face, feeling the heat of embarrassment crawl up her neck. "Mrs. Williams, I'm not planning on marrying. It's not for me."

"Huh," Mrs. Williams said, placing an elbow on the table and resting her chin in her hand. "I thought for sure something was going on between you and Micah here." The older woman wiggled her finger between her and Micah.

*Lord, call me home, please.*

"Mrs. Williams, Belle and I are friends and colleagues." Micah's deep voice seemed to reverberate in the room.

"Micah dear, you're not getting any younger. You're too good of a man to remain single."

"Mother!" Dwight and Delaney exclaimed.

The older woman threw her hands up. "What? Is honesty a sin now?"

"More like inserting your foot in your mouth is." Luke's lips quirked in amusement.

"I can't help it if I just want people to be happy."

Belle couldn't believe it. The older woman sat back in her chair, her arms folded. Her eyes took on the characteristics of a puppy who'd been kicked.

"Happiness is different for everyone, Mrs. Williams," Belle offered. "I recently took up crocheting. Maybe you need a hobby."

"Yes!" Nina, Dwight, Luke, and Delaney exclaimed.

Silence froze the table's patrons.

"Fine," she snapped out. "I get the point. You all want me to butt out."

"We say it with love, Ma," Dwight said. He nuzzled his face in Gabe's neck, sending happy giggles in the air.

Envy stabbed her heart like an ice pick. Despite the past, this is what she wanted. A family who would love no matter what. People to sit around with and do life with. A fellowship of the deepest kind.

And maybe, just maybe a man to complete the picture.

Unbidden, she turned and startled, finding Micah's piercing gaze watching her. His obsidian eyes seemed to hypnotize her. She couldn't have looked away unless a major-disaster alarm sounded.

"See, the food is worth it, isn't it?" He asked softly.

*And the family.* She looked at her plate, realizing she ate most of it. "Definitely."

The conversation continued at a more sedate pace. Gone was the frantic noise of hungry children and complaining adults. Fun and laughter filtered around the table drawing them close in friendship and harmony.

Belle tried to finish the rest of her food at a slower pace. When Mrs. Williams brought out dessert, she savored each bite, trying to prolong the moment. She hoped this day would last in her memory bank for years to come. After the hospital incident, she needed more good days to store up. Next to accepting Christ as her Savior, there weren't that many.

If she could have more moments like this, maybe life wouldn't be so hard. Maybe she could continue to work, find a hobby that she could enjoy and recreate herself. She owed it to herself to discover who she could be in Christ. As the Pastor reminded her today, her sins had been washed away.

*Lord, please let it be so. I want to forget my sins. I'm tired of the weight of carrying it around. I want to be forgiven, I'm just not sure what that looks like. I know I can't go back to my old behavior, but who am I outside of that?*

*Please show me, Amen.*

༄

Micah sat on his deck, while Noodles explored his aviary. The screened-in structure housed some climbing apparatuses, a food bowl, and provided space to fly around and enjoy the fresh air without fear of predators. Noodles happily hopped from branch to branch. Micah glanced at his watch. Since the temperatures were getting lower, he didn't want to stay out too long. Just enough for his friend to get some fresh air.

He pulled his cell phone out of his coat pocket and dialed his father.

"Hello, son."

The distinctive voice of his pop washed over him. People always told his father he could be a voice actor. "Hey, Pop. How are you?"

"Not too shabby."

Micah stared at his nails. Now that he had his father on the phone, he wasn't really sure what to say. Usually he had no problem thinking of a conversation starter.

"What's bugging you, son?"

"What isn't?" His head drooped.

"Loaded question. Expand. Tell me what's going on."

Micah laughed. He could always count on his dad to add levity to the situation. "Where to start?"

"At the beginning. The Bible starts there, so I figure that's a good rule of thumb."

"Ha. Thanks a lot, Pop."

"You asked."

"What was I thinking?"

"That your old man is wise beyond his years and could help you out of your girl trouble?"

He stared at the phone in shock. The sound of his father cackling, filtered through the roar in his ears. "Girl trouble? What makes you think I have girl trouble?"

"The silence that greeted me when I said it." His dad snorted. "Seriously, I didn't fall off the turnip truck yesterday. Women always have a way of stealing your words."

"I don't know what to do about her."

"Give me some background, son."

So, he did. Micah told his father how he felt when Belle first started working and how he felt now—and everything in between. When he finished, he leaned back in his chair. Suddenly, the noose didn't seem so tight.

"Seems like you've been thinking and praying about this a lot."

"Trying to."

"Good. Prayer is the first and last thing we should do, son. Have you thought of just having fun without overanalyzing it? You want to hang out with her? Do it. Want to ask her to grab a cup of coffee? Go ahead. You young kids make dating too complicated."

He was pushing forty, young had left the building. And dating. Dating wasn't a word he'd use, but then again, maybe that did make it too complicated. "I promised to be a good friend."

"Then be one. I'm beginning to feel like I'm talking to a brick wall. Life's really not that complicated. You pray, seek guidance, and put feet to what God's calling you to do. You think He wants you to be a friend, then act accordingly. Friends get together. Share their hopes and dreams. Keep the romance out, and you'll be fine. I'm sure she'll let you know if she wants the status to change."

"What if I want it to?"

"Did God tell you to change it?"

*Ouch. That burned a little.* "No, He didn't."

"Then there's your answer."

"All right, Pop." He rubbed the back of his head.

"Now, when are you going to come and visit? Your mom's moping around here talking about her only child hasn't visited in eons. I think I saw a tear or two leak out."

"Don't be lying on me, Jeremiah Campbell," his mom yelled in the background.

"Then who said it, Evelyn?"

"You, you ol' coot."

His father chuckled, the laugh rumbling in his throat. "God love your mother, son."

"And you love her too."

"You can't prove it. Now, Micah, you get off this phone, and call that young lady friend of yours. Take her out. Have fun. And please stop thinking so much."

"I'll see what I can do."

"And stop by before Christmas rolls around when you're obligated to do so."

"Yes, Pop."

Micah stood, sliding his cell in his pocket. He walked over to the aviary, where Noodles sat perched on a branch near an empty bowl. "Inside, Noodles?"

"Brrr," he squawked.

"Agreed." He opened the aviary and walked in, then stretched out his hand.

Carefully, Noodles grabbed on with his talons. When his friend was steady, Micah moved his hand close to his chest and headed inside. The African grey snuggled close, rubbing his head against his chest in affection.

"Brrr," Noodles repeated.

"Hopefully, the winter will be short, buddy."

Last year had been absolutely frigid in Bethesda. He knew from the news that the northern part of Virginia had been worse. So far, this year remained tolerable. It was cold, but no temperatures in the teens or lower due to wind chill.

Micah placed Noodles back in his cage and draped a sheet over it for night time. With a sigh, he headed for his library, the favorite place in his home. Quiet, filled with books and the book scent that went hand in hand. Also, his chosen place to talk to God.

*Wonder what Belle is up to?*

If he had her number, he'd call. Only, he'd talked himself out of getting it. Was his pop right? Had he been thinking too hard? As much as he wanted life to be simple, it wasn't. Not for him. He'd begun to desire something more than friendship with Belle. Micah struggled to keep that in mind every time he was near her.

*Lord Father, help me walk the path You've set before me. I know You called me to be patient. Please keep me in that lane and nothing else, unless You say so. In Jesus' Name, Amen.*

## 9

Belle felt like skipping. Ever since church and lunch with the Williams family, she'd been riding on high. Life was finally looking up. She felt like God was trying to reassure her that she could have a normal, happy life. That her sins wouldn't dictate her present or future. Up until now, she'd been pretty sure that the consequences of her actions were too difficult to overcome.

But no one in Maple Run knew her past.

She truly had a fresh start and an escape from Garrett. *Garrett.* Chills crawled up her arm, leaving goosebumps in their wake. As of last week, she no longer had ties to him. That lovely divorce certificate gave her a lease on a new life. One without fear. She'd thought about going back to her maiden name, but that would raise more questions than she wanted. Instead, she would continue to be Belle Peterson, even if the Peterson last name haunted her dreams.

*Don't fear.* He had no idea where she was. Like always, the thought of Garrett brought an unease that didn't shake quite so easily. She tried to grasp onto the joy she had before her thoughts took a downward turn.

*Please, bring all my thoughts captive under the obedience of the Lord*

*Jesus Christ. Strike Garrett from my mind. And thank You for freeing me.*

Never had she been so happy to be a divorced woman. It would have never been an option before, but when a man left lasting marks, safety became paramount. Even if she was the cause of him crossing the line.

*You're free, Belle. Let go of him and everything that happened.*

She could do this. Live a redeemed life and serve God with joy. After all He'd done for her, why wouldn't she? *I promise to be joyful today, Lord. No looking back, just forward.*

With a smile, she opened her car door and headed for the employee entrance to the family practice. Her steps quickened as the wind chilled her skin, but when a flutter of white crossed her vision, she slowed to a stop. She looked up in the sky and gasped.

"It's snowing." She held out a glove hand and marveled as a thick flake landed on it.

"Belle, get out of the snow."

She turned and saw Mimi gesture inside the door way. Hurrying she joined the older woman. "Morning, Mimi."

"Morning. What were you doing standing out there? Trying to catch pneumonia?"

"No," she chuckled. "A snowflake. It's absolutely gorgeous." She stared down into her hand, disappointment filled her. The snowflake had dissolved.

"Well, thankfully the weatherman said it'll pass in an hour. I'm not ready for the heavy stuff."

"Never paid attention to the weather until I moved here. Does it snow a lot?"

"Seems like the last few years we've gotten more and more snow. We even got the tail end of a blizzard last year. Clinic had to close for a few days."

"Blizzard?" Her toes wiggled in fear in her boots.

"Yes, ma'am. You weren't bargaining for that, were you?"

"Not really."

"Don't worry, Belle. You'll have plenty of opportunities to catch snowflakes if a blizzard comes."

The rest of the morning went by fast. As predicted, the snow went away after an hour. Belle stared out the front window, sad the flurries had faded. No evidence remained to indicate it had snowed earlier. Maybe it would do so for Christmas. She could build a snowman and put a crocheted scarf around him.

Her thoughts drifted to the gift bag Ms. Mable had sent. It still remained untouched on her kitchen countertop. Belle just couldn't bring herself to dabble in jewelry making. She didn't want anything to suck her back into her old way of life. It was bad enough she lost the beauty of clothes. Experimenting with jewelry creation would only aggravate the wound more. She stared down at her wrist. The one that had required all sorts of hardware to be put back together. The one that had been crushed with blows from a man too strong for his own good.

It certainly hadn't been for her own good. Then again, she wouldn't have met Cara Smith if she hadn't been in the hospital. The woman had saved her life and shared the good news of Jesus Christ. She'd always be grateful to her. If only it hadn't taken so much to bring her to her knees in humility.

Hindsight had to be the most painful part of life. Except, she was tired of living in the sea of what-ifs. It was time to embrace the joy God offered her. The freedom from sin. *Lord, I accept your offer. Please show me how to live this life for Your glory.*

"Thinking awfully hard over there."

She turned and smiled up at Micah. "Just in a contemplative mood."

"Want to share?" He met her gaze, his hands resting in his slacks' pockets. There was no curiosity shining in his eyes, only simple patience.

Her heart turned over. "Maybe some other time."

"Definitely." He paused. "I was wondering if you wanted to

grab a bite to eat after work? Rumor has it something new is on The Pit's menu."

Indecision chased away her words.

"Just as friends, Belle."

"I know." *Or rather she had hoped.* "That sounds like fun," she hedged. *Why was it so hard to accept his offer?* "Mrs. Williams is going to make me gain weight if I eat at The Pit too often."

"I think that's her mission in life." Micah said, white teeth gleaming.

A puff of disappointment escaped her lips. She thought for sure he'd make some comment about her figure. Yet, he stuck to his good-friends campaign.

*Wasn't that what she wanted?*

"I still can't get that bread pudding out of my mind. I think I may have had a sugar induced dream about it last night."

Micah doubled over. "When I was in the military on deployment, I always had dreams about Twinkies."

"Twinkies?"

"You couldn't get them over there. I had to wait until my..." A look of unease crossed his face. "I had to wait until I got a care package with them. As soon as I had one...or two," he said with a wink. "The dreams stopped."

"That's hilarious. How often do you eat them now?"

"Oh, whenever I see some in stock. You should see what's in my deep freezer."

The image brought a chuckle forth. "So, Twinkies are your food weakness?"

"Yes, ma'am. Yours?"

"Oreos. Double stuffed."

"Favorite food?"

"Gnocchi, freshly made."

Micah grinned. "With or without garlic bread?"

Her nose wrinkled. "No, garlic bread, but a nice sourdough with rosemary and olive oil to dip it in."

The pressure to be a beauty faded away in the face of his friendship and easy conversation. Her mother wasn't there to encourage her to catch an available rich male. Talking with Micah allowed her to simply be herself. The girl who loved double-stuffed Oreos and all things dessert-related.

"My bird got a hold of a Twinkie once."

"You have a bird?"

"African grey parrot."

"Oh, those are beautiful. They're the ones with the bright red tail feathers, right?"

"Yes." He looked surprised. "You like birds?"

"I'm not sure. I've been doing internet searches trying to figure out what kind of pet I want."

"You want a pet?"

*I don't want to be alone.* "Maybe."

"Birds are great companions."

"So are cats," Mimi called out.

"You know," Micah said with a snap of his fingers. "Shorty mentioned something about needing a home for a cat. I could take you there to check it out, if you want."

Be alone with him? He'd never been improper, but that didn't stop her stomach from fluttering. "Uh...sure."

"Okay, then. And dinner? As friends?"

Belle nodded slowly.

"Okay then." Micah smiled at her and tipped an imaginary hat before walking toward the exam rooms. She stared after him, her brow wrinkling in confusion. Something interesting just happened. Only, she wasn't sure what.

ஃ

Today had turned out to be a good day. Micah smiled to himself as he typed up his patient notes. Belle had been particularly cheerful all day. He couldn't believe how open she had been about her love for Oreos and other desserts. Perhaps Pop was right. All he needed to do was talk to her like a friend, and everything else would fall into place. That was the longest he'd talked to her in one setting.

For once, the shadows seemed to be permanently gone from her eyes. Instead, they had sparkled with peace and joy. And heightened the spark of attraction he felt.

*Patience is a virtue, Campbell.*

Maybe if he kept telling himself that, he'd eventually believe it. He had first-hand knowledge that knowing something and *practicing* it were as different as the flu and common cold. The promise to be a good friend remained like a noose around his neck. It couldn't be ignored. If he did...who knew what would happen. Nothing good ever happened when he bypassed patience. It was a hard lesson but one he intended on learning. *Please guide me, Lord. Help me let patience bring about my endurance.*

He took out his cell and zipped a text to Shorty.

*You still need a home for the cat?*

*Yes. U interested?*

*No, but Belle might be.*

*Great! Can she come by sometime this week and see him?*

*I'll ask and get back to you.*

He finished typing the last patient's notes. Belle had gone home to change out of her scrubs. Something about washing the day's germs off her. He had about five more minutes before he needed to head home and do the same. Noodles would squawk his displeasure if he didn't hurry.

On the way home and throughout Noodle's feeding routine, Micah prayed that the evening would go well. As he headed for The Pit, a twinge of unease filtered through him. He felt awful for not picking Belle up, but she insisted on meeting him at the restaurant. If she were a male friend, there wouldn't be an issue, about meeting one another at a restaurant. Guys didn't drive together to hang out. But she was a woman, a very beautiful one at that. Somehow, he didn't think she'd appreciate him pointing that out.

He parked his SUV and headed inside. Nikki stood there, grinning from behind the hostess' stand.

"Hey, Micah. You joining Belle?"

"Yes. Where is she?" He scanned the crowd and saw her at the bar.

Definitely not a date. Friends sat at barstools and dates sat in the cozy looking tables for two. He glanced down at his jeans and sweater. Not like he dressed for a date anyway. Praying he could keep his cool, he walked over to Belle.

"Did you order?" He sat down on her right.

"Just coffee. I ordered one for you. Hope that's okay?"

"Perfect, thanks." He tapped his hands on the countertop. *Just a friend. A good friend.* "Shorty says you can come by any time this week to meet the cat."

"Okay. How about Wednesday?"

"Why Wednesday?" His brow furrowed as he looked at her, trying not to be suckered in by her gorgeous eyes. Gorgeous eyes —and long lashes that framed them perfectly.

"Nothing comes on TV."

He laughed. "I didn't realize you watched so much TV."

"Crocheting allows me to watch TV and keep my hands occupied. Not sure what else I should be doing." She shrugged.

"I hear ya. Other than hanging with my bird and the guys occasionally, I'm at odds of how to fill my time."

"Is that sad? Do you think other people our age wander around aimlessly? Shouldn't we be more driven?"

He raised an eyebrow. "I don't think you're in my age bracket." *But not too far off,* he hoped. Feeling old had been happening since he hit thirty. No need to dig the knife in deeper.

"Unless you're in your forties, we're in the same bracket."

"You're in your thirties?"

She nodded. "Just hit thirty."

"You're a baby." He nudged her with his elbow.

"You?"

"Thirty-eight."

"Ah, an old man." She nodded as if his age explained everything.

A bark of laughter escaped. "Ouch, you wound me."

"Sure, I did."

"You ever been married?"

Belle stiffened beside him.

*Wrong question?* The tension coming off her practically crackled the air. Did he push or tell his story to take the heat off her? "I was."

"What happened?" Her voice came out more quiet than usual. Caution laced her words.

"She couldn't handle the amount of time I dedicated to the Army."

She gazed at him. "And?"

He broke her stare, not wanting to see the look of pity when he told her. "She cheated on me with my cousin."

A soft gasp met his ears. "That's awful."

"It was. I was pretty mad at the whole female populous for a while."

"Rightly so."

He turned, but she stared at the countertop. Her voice sounded so mournful. "Hey, you okay?"

She shrugged. "Marriage is a terrible thing. All it does is tear you into two."

"Nah, look at Nina and Dwight. It's only made them better."

"One in a million."

"My parents have been married over forty years."

"Okay, two in a million."

"Don't forget about Dwight's parents."

A sigh fell from her lips. "My parents are divorced. My father's been remarried four times. My mother...I stopped counting."

*Ouch.* That wasn't going to help his argument any. "Not every marriage ends in divorce."

"Mine did."

Shock paralyzed him. She'd been married? Was it her husband who'd hurt her? The thought made him cringe. A man should cherish his wife, not harm her. "What happened?"

"I don't want to talk about it." She sat up straight. "I'm not that hungry. Maybe we can have a rain check?" She stood.

"Belle, wait."

The shadows had returned. The light and sparkle that had filled her eyes today had vanished.

"You don't have to say anything, Micah. It is what it is and sometimes it's our fault."

With that, she walked away, leaving him to attempt to decipher her cryptic remarks.

## 10

The joy of the previous day remained elusive. No matter how much Belle repeated Scripture in her head, peace remained outside her reach. Instead, Micah's words reverberated in her head like a clanging symbol. *"She cheated on me with my cousin."*

Each remembrance was like a pounding headache. Whatever chance she thought she had with him evaporated with that admission. There was no way he would date a woman who did the same thing to her spouse. Nausea swirled in the pit of her stomach. The kind that refused to be eradicated with ginger or anti-nausea medication.

She was a cheater.

An adulteress.

Not worthy of forgiveness or love.

*But Jesus forgave you.*

She squeezed her eyes tight and a tear slipped free. How could she reconcile her warring thoughts? The devil and the angel were very real, constantly whispering in her ear. But who declared the loudest?

The Bible insisted she was pure as snow, but she saw the look of disgust in Micah's eyes when he mentioned his ex-wife, who was no different from her. And now she knew a life of solitude would be her penitence.

"Why does my heart have to pound every time he's around, Lord? This is torture."

The words echoed in her apartment, still devoid of pictures and other embellishments. Saved people weren't materialistic. At least, that's what she told herself each time she passed by pretty things. Once, her life had revolved around any possession she could get her hands on. It had eased the ache of depression that haunted her the moment she said, "I do."

Oh, she'd known Garrett Peterson cared more about himself than he did her when they dated, but her mother had encouraged the relationship. After all, if someone else could keep her in the affluence she'd been raised in, the better. So, her mother said, especially since it took the strain off her income—more for her mother to spend.

Garrett's vanity never bothered her. While they dated and during their engagement, he made sure to pay proper homage to her looks while keeping his eyes fastened on his. No, his ego certainly hadn't bothered her. Instead, the subtle way he insulted her after they married had dug under her skin. Too bad his subtly didn't last. Her mind went back to the night she knew her ex-husband wasn't as charming as he portrayed. A couple of months after their wedding, his true colors had been revealed.

"Belle, why did you put the towels here?" Garrett motioned to the hall closet.

She stared at it a moment and then him. *Was this a trick question?* "They're clean."

"I should hope so. If you're folding dirty towels, then we have bigger problems than I thought."

"Okay." The word came out slow.

"Ugh." His top lip curled in disdain, his brow furrowing over his beady, black eyes. "Do you *see* how far this is from our bathroom?"

Unease skittered up her spine. Garrett could be rude, but there was an underlying emotion she couldn't quite put her finger on. "Garrett, it's right down the hall." She motioned. "Plus, this is the linen closet."

His hand snaked out, grabbing her chin in a tight squeeze. "You talking smart?"

"No," her voice wavered, fear speeding up her pulse. Pinpoints of tension pricked her underarms, while her stomach rolled with fright. She swallowed. "I just meant there's no place to put the towels in our room."

He pushed her head back, letting her chin go. "Put them in our closet."

"Where?" She resisted the urge to rub her chin. The mutinous expression on his face terrified her. He'd never looked at her that way before. Mild annoyance: yes. Hatred: no.

"I suggest you move all those jeans cluttering your side. There's no reason to have so many."

"And put them where?"

He stared at the linen closet then at her, his arms folded.

An inhale.

A heartbeat.

"Are we clear?"

"Yes, Garrett."

Belle wiped away a tear at the memory. She'd called her mother once he had showered and left for a business meeting. One where she hadn't been needed to smile and look pretty on his arm. When she tried to relay the terror that had coursed through her, her mother merely brushed her off.

"Belle, stop being dramatic. Husbands are very particular when it comes to their homes. It's where they unwind after a taxing day. You don't work, so you have no idea the pressure they're under."

*Because Garrett forbade me to join the workforce.* And now she was wasting her nursing degree. The one her mother had objected to. No wonder she wanted Belle to be a housewife. "But, Mother."

"No buts, Belle. You get your house in order. Set it up the way your husband wants, and you won't have any problems."

"He hurt me." She rushed the words out before her mother could hang up on her.

"Sweetie, you can't come crying to me every time your feelings get hurt. Work it out."

A click and empty space followed.

Her mother had hung up.

By the time Garrett came home that night, he'd been in high spirits. Apparently, his business meeting had been a success. He'd come home smelling of cigars and a touch of alcohol. The pair of diamond earrings he gave her were the first of many apologies.

Not that he ever uttered the word 'sorry.'

She snorted. Garrett Peterson wouldn't know remorse if it hung from his torso sucking the life from him like a leech.

A knock interrupted her musings.

*Who could that be?*

Another knock. "Coming."

Her mental calendar popped up. *Wednesday evening.* Did she have something scheduled? She stood on her toes and saw Micah through the peep hole.

*The cat.*

Quickly, she unlocked the door. "Hey."

"Ready to go see the cat?"

She looked down at her loose-fitting jogging outfit. Should she change? *You don't want to attract his attention anyway.* True, especially knowing what she did about his divorce.

"Sure, let me grab by purse."

A minute later, Micah held the car door open for her as she got into his SUV. Her objection to follow him in her own car had been overridden. The hair on her arms stood up as he slid behind the wheel. The scent of his cologne teased her senses.

But it always did.

Every time he walked by her at work, her body leaned forward on its own accord. If she were a cartoon, she'd be lifted off her feet by now, following his tantalizing scent around the office. But how could she ignore the woodsy scent curling around her like a warm sweater? *Time to stop thinking, Belle.*

"Whose house are we going to again?"

"Shorty's. He's Dwight's best friend and my friend by association."

"Shorty?"

"His last name is Smalls."

"Men and their nicknames."

"What? You don't like Soup?" His eyes twinkled, his lips twitching with laughter.

"No." She said with a straight face. "Hate the stuff."

"Ouch." He touched his chest. "Maybe you just haven't tried the right one."

Her mouth dropped open.

"Sorry." A look of chagrin crossed his face. "I didn't mean it the way it came out. I..." His hands faltered, searching for what, she wasn't sure.

Was it fair to make the man so uncomfortable for innocent banter? *But, you know where that leads.*

*Not with him.* "It's all right." She exhaled. "I'm not ultrasensitive." Of course she was, but he didn't have to know that.

"Yes, but..."

"But what?"

"I just wanted to show you I can be a friend."

"Friends joke, Micah. Besides, we both know nothing more will ever happen, so stop worrying."

*"We both know nothing more will ever happen."*

The words stung, because deep down, he wanted something to happen. He wanted Belle to give him a chance in the romance department. It was part of the reason he had been willing to be patient. Part of the reason he put himself out there when self-preservation tried to yank him back.

*So, you just want to be a friend until it benefits you.*

Ouch. He ran a hand across his jaw.

"What's wrong?"

"Just thinking." He stared out the windshield, as he turned down the street toward Shorty's home.

The man lived a few miles away from Belle's apartment, in one of the more established neighborhoods of Maple Run. The houses all looked different and each had a few acres of land.

"Want to talk about it, friend?"

*Just pour the salt in.* How could he tell her his thoughts? It would negate all the talk he said about friendship. *And make the rejection all the sweeter...not.* "I better not. I'll work through it."

He looked at her, but she quickly averted her gaze. A sigh slipped from his lips. "Belle, it's not you."

"It's me?" She shook her head, a sardonic expression twisting her beautiful lips into something dark. "I thought friends told the truth."

"I can't." He squeezed the steering wheel, trying to focus on the mailbox numbers, looking for Shorty's place. "Words can't be taken back, Belle. Once they're released...it's over."

"Oh, and 'it's not you' is a phrase you want to let fly?"

"Better than saying 'Belle, I want you to be my girlfriend.'"

Micah braked. He wanted to close his eyes or better yet, disappear. Why did he say that out loud?

The number on the mailbox nearest him matched the address Shorty texted him. He backed up to park in the driveway.

Silence filled the interior of his SUV. Could he pretend like he didn't just break his promise of being patient? Of putting his feelings out there? He should have just kept his mouth shut, but no, Belle had to turn those cat-shaped eyes his way with a look that seared straight to his heart.

Defenses were down.

Words flew.

And now he had to deal with the awful silence. He slowly turned to look at her.

Tears filled her eyes and remained unshed but turned her dark eyes luminous. "You want to date me?" She whispered, but the silence in the car allowed the sound to ring loud and clear to his fast-beating heart.

"Belle," he murmured. *Yes.* He wanted to shout. Micah swallowed. "I think right now we should just be friends."

She licked her lips. "But you want me to be your girlfriend?" A tear slipped down her cheek, but before she could wipe her face, his thumb erased the evidence of her turmoil.

"Yes, I do, but I can tell you've been hurt before. I can be patient." His lips quirked up. "Despite evidence to the contrary." He *would* be patient if it killed him...which most likely it would.

"Micah, you deserve someone better than me. I can't be what you need."

*Can't or won't?* Fear and longing warred on her face. She turned her eyes downward, avoiding his gaze.

*Tap, tap.*

Micah startled, turning toward his window. Shorty grinned, making a motion to roll down the window. He pressed the button release.

"You guys coming in or are you going to continue loitering in my driveway?"

"We're coming." Micah forced a chuckle, hoping to dispel some of the tension lingering in the cab. He opened the door and gave Shorty a fist bump. Belle came around the SUV and stood next to him. "Shorty, this is Belle. Belle, Shorty."

"Nice to meet you, pretty lady." Shorty shook her hand and offered a harmless grin. "The cat's been waiting."

"Does he have a name?" Belle asked, arms folded across her chest.

Was she still thinking about his confession? He followed behind her as Shorty lead them to the side door entrance to his garage.

"I call him 'the cat.'" He unlocked the door. "He seems to prefer the garage. Probably all the sawdust."

Micah quirked an eyebrow. Cats liked sawdust?

"What's with the sawdust?" Belle asked.

"See for yourself." Shorty gestured inside.

Belle walked inside, and Micah heard her gasp. Curious, he followed behind her and stopped. Furniture filled the garage. He stepped close, examining an unfinished dining table. "You made this?"

Shorty nodded. "Kind of a hobby."

"What a wonderful hobby." Belle ran a hand along a dresser. "It's gorgeous."

"Thank you," Shorty said.

"Man, I had no idea." Micah examined a writing desk. "Do you sell these?"

"I do. I just don't advertise." He shrugged, as if embarrassed. "Anyway, the cat likes to hide here." He pointed to another dining table, a fresh layer of sawdust underneath. A gray Persian lay on his back, his paws in the air.

"What a gorgeous cat. He's a stray?" Belle turned her beguiling eyes toward Shorty.

*Man is she gorgeous.* Couple that with her sweet personality, and it stood the reason why attraction spiked whenever she was near. The sadness in her eyes hit him right in the heart.

"Yes, ma'am. I made the mistake of giving him milk, and now he's taken up residence. But, I'm gone a lot. Not home long enough to care for a cat."

"Where do you go?" The words slipped out before Micah realized how nosy they were.

"Furniture delivery."

"Some hobby, Shorty."

Shorty looked away then pointed toward Belle. She'd scooped the cat up, nestling it against her chest.

"He's so soft," she murmured.

The cat purred, stretching its head against her. It licked the side of her face in affection.

"Lucky cat," he murmured.

Shorty snickered, then coughed. "You want him?"

"I...achoo." Belle winced as the sneeze tore through her. Then another one. And another.

"Uh, Belle, you might want to let the cat go?" Micah pointed. "Your skin's getting red." Her skin was turning red on her cheek.

Her mouth dropped open and she set down the cat. She examined her hands. "I'm allergic?"

"Looks like." He stepped closer, triaging her symptoms. "Can you breathe?"

She nodded.

"Stick out your tongue."

Belle complied.

"You might just need some over-the-counter allergy meds. Come on, I'll take you to the store." He turned toward Shorty. "Looks like you have a cat, man. Might want to give him a better name though."

Shorty picked up the cat. "Sorry, Belle."

"No worries. I didn't know."

They cut their good-byes short as Micah escorted Belle out into the night.

## 11

The mall was jam packed. It had taken Delaney a half hour to find a parking spot. Belle looked around, taking in the sights before her. People filled the walkway between the stores. Others filed out of said places, joining the throng of people in the middle.

"I can't believe all the people," she whispered.

"It's like this every holiday season," Nikki intoned.

"Really?"

"Really." Delaney, Nina, and Nikki parroted.

Belle laughed. "I guess so then."

"Where to first?" Dee asked.

Nina named a boutique. "I want to buy a dress for the Christmas festival."

"Oh, good idea. I almost forgot that was next week." Dee clasped her hands together. "You going Nikki? Belle?" She looked at each one of them.

*Not if I can help it.* Why go to a festival if she couldn't dress up and feel pretty?

"Probably," Nikki said. "I always have fun."

"Belle?" Nina asked, peeking around the other ladies.

"I'll pass." She tried to infuse a lightness that wasn't there, while her pulse pounded in her throat.

"But why?" Nikki asked. "The town does such a wonderful job of putting it together. There's food, music, wonderful decorations." Nikki smiled. "There's even dancing."

"No one to dance with." She shrugged, but knew it was a lie. What would it be like to have Micah wrap his arms around her? His proclamation the other day still beat in her heart.

"At the risk of sounding like my mother," Dee said wryly. "What about Micah?"

Belle had to resist the urge to shrug under their scrutiny. "I don't know if he's going, but it doesn't matter." They entered the boutique and Belle paused.

Racks of clothes filled the interior, with fashionable mannequins stationed here and there. Longing filled her heart. The desire to put on a dress and twirl, just because she could, flooded her senses. She looked up and noticed that the ladies had drifted apart, each perusing a different rack.

*There's no harm in looking, right?*

Belle swallowed and blindly headed toward one of the racks. A few flicks of her wrist and she realized they were skirts. Skirts that flared out so one could twirl. A sharp inhale stole her breath as she picked one up in her size. Tentatively, she held it in front of her as her imagination danced in delight. The cream-colored skirt had streaks of color running down like artwork. And there were pockets. *Pockets!*

*Oh, Lord, You know I can't resist pockets. Why can't I have pretty things?*

"That's gorgeous," Nikki said. She beamed at Belle. "That would be perfect to dance in at the Christmas festival," Nikki said with a sing-song tone.

Longing pulled at her. The skirt did have the twirl factor. She fingered the fabric, loving the softness against her skin. Her fingers dipped into the pockets.

"It has pockets?" Nikki cried out. "Perfect! I'm a sucker for a skirt with pockets."

"Everything's better with them."

"Amen."

Belle stared at the tag. It *was* within her budget. It's not like she spent her money frivolously these days.

"What's stopping you?" Nikki asked.

"Don't you think it's too much?"

"The price?"

"No," she shook her head. "Too much for a Christian."

"What's too much?" Nina asked, as she and Delaney walked over.

Heat filled her cheeks as the ladies eyed her in confusion. "Don't you think Christians shouldn't be ostentatious in their outfits? We aren't supposed to call attention to ourselves, right?" She stared at the women, hoping one of them understood her plight.

"Have you heard of the Proverbs 31 woman?" Nikki asked.

"No." She had no clue where to start reading in the Bible. Sixty-six books were a little intimidating. Instead, she found verses from Bible devotionals and memorized them.

"She's the perfect woman," Delaney added. "But one thing I remember was that she dressed nicely. Made the clothes herself."

"Exactly," Nikki smiled. "You're right, Belle. We don't have to draw needless attention to ourselves. But it's not like this skirt is a skin-tight-barely-cover-your-rear-end advertisement. Plus, if you're shopping with godliness in mind, I'm sure He'll guide you if you just ask."

Was that true? Confusion wrinkled her brow. "There was a time when I only cared about appearances. I never left home without makeup. Only shopped designer brands, and I was a shameless flirt." *By design or creation?* Did it matter? Her voice trailed, as she remembered her despicable actions. Why couldn't she have met the Lord before then? "I don't want to get sucked into that lifestyle again."

"What's changed since then?" Nina asked, concern softening her facial features.

"I found God."

"Hallelujah," Dee said. "He makes a difference."

"Only you can decide what you can or cannot handle." Nina offered. "But don't let fear keep you from the abundant life He's promised you."

Belle blinked. The clarity of Nina's words rang true. She never asked God about the materialistic aspect of her past life. Instead, she purged her life of all things beautiful because of fear. She didn't want to put herself in another compromising position like the one that ended up with her in the hospital. It's why she ignored the way her pulse skittered in Micah's presence...well as best as she could.

"I hear what you're saying." She eyed the skirt.

*Do I, Lord?*

No response. She bit her lip. "I think I want to try it on."

"Here." Nikki thrust a taupe top at her. "Try this on with it."

"Thanks."

The ladies followed her to the dressing room. As she changed into the skirt and blouse, her mind reeled. Could she dress in feminine clothing and not be considered a flirt? An image of the electronics employee popped into her mind. She'd been wearing jeans and a puffer jacket and that wasn't enough to dissuade him.

*Some men are like that.*

She shuddered, indecision freezing her to the spot.

"Come on out, Belle," Dee called out.

If she opened her eyes and saw her reflection, would the look be too much for her to handle? Making a decision, she opened the dressing room door, bypassing the mirror. Slowly, she opened her eyes and stood still.

Nikki, Nina, and Delaney stared at her in shock.

"Do I look horrible?"

"You didn't look?" Nikki asked. Her red ponytail swung as if to punctuate her question.

"Too chicken."

"Well, come here." Nikki pulled her to a mirror in the waiting area. "You look just as beautiful as your name implies."

Her reflection shocked her. She still had the prominent cheek bones, perfectly arched eyebrows, and full lips. Despite the lack of makeup, she felt beautiful. Was it the clothes? Sure, the taupe shirt fit comfortably into her waistband, courtesy of her nightly crunches. The way the skirt flared away begged her to do a little spin.

"I don't know, you guys. I haven't been this dressed up in..." *Four months, three days, and ten hours, but who's counting?*

"It's not like you're planning on seducing anyone," Nina quipped.

The blood drained from her face.

Nina must have noticed because the smile fell from her face. "I'm just joking, Belle."

"Sure," she choked out. Only there was a little bit of truth in every joke, wasn't there? Did they think she would try and seduce their men? She wasn't like that. Had only been like that because...

"I'm going to go take this off." She turned around, hoping no one noticed the tears springing up.

"Belle, wait." Nina stopped her as she reached the door to the fitting room. "Do you need to talk?" she murmured.

Belle stared at Nina. She wanted a friend, had always wanted a friend, but females always saw her as a threat. No one wanted to be friends with the too pretty, rich girl. They were always afraid she'd stab them in the back and called her names when they thought she wasn't around.

Yet, Nina had showed none of those traits. Could she share her secret, or would Nina run the other way?

"You can trust me." Nina turned and motioned for Nikki and Delaney to leave.

Belle couldn't see exactly what she did or said, but heard retreating footsteps. Nina turned back around. "You need to talk before you explode."

"I cheated on my husband."

Nina blinked. "You're married?"

"Was," she rushed out. She folded her arms around her waist. *Why is it freezing in here?*

"Let's sit down."

Thankfully, her dressing room had two chairs. Higher-end boutiques always made sure their clientele was comfortable, she thought in the back of her mind.

"What happened?"

"My ex is a business man. He was all about impressing the men he dealt with. It was one of the reasons he chose to marry me. Said I looked good on his arm." She looked down, recalling how the words had pierced her soul. It was one thing to think you were arm candy, another to have it confirmed.

"Anyway," she breathed out. "He didn't mind if I flirted. Said it helped relax the clients. He even—" no she couldn't go there. She ran a hand over her face.

"Go on," Nina gently prodded.

"After we married he stopped the charming behavior. Began chastising me as if I were a child."

Nina sat straighter. "What do you mean chastised you?" Her words came out slowly, laced with an emotion Belle couldn't identify.

"First it was just words then…"

Nina placed a hand on her arm.

Drawing courage from her touch, she forged ahead. "He gave me a black eye."

Horror flared in Nina's brown eyes.

Shame heated Belle's cheeks. "Nina—"

"Wait, just a minute," she said softly. "I'm sure you're wondering what I'm thinking since my face is kind of expressive."

"Not really," she lied. Why would she want to know how little Nina thought of her?

"Belle, it's not your fault."

"Yes, it is." She whipped out. "He was my husband. I knew exactly what he was capable of. Had the bruising and memories to remind myself of what he could do. When he told me he needed my help for an important dinner, I was too scared to object. And I took it too far." Her breath came in spurts, as the horror of that night came back.

"What did he do?" Nina whispered.

&

The sun shined on the Chesapeake Bay, sparkling in its splendor. Micah couldn't help but think of God's creation. It constantly amazed Him that God had trusted man to look after earth. And it shamed him to realize how they mistreated it. Yet, on this part of the bay, you could still see the purity in the water.

Micah turned into the senior condo community where his parents lived. He parked, locked his door, and headed for their first-floor condo. As he neared, smells of a savory meal hovered around the door. He sniffed trying to detect what his mother was making.

Before he could knock, the door swung wide open.

"Micah, my boy." His father grinned.

His dad's hair had turned completely white about ten years ago. His brown skin was covered with moles around his cheeks. Micah bit back a laugh at the floral-patterned shirt that his father wore. It was reminiscent of a Hawaiian vacation instead of December in Annapolis. "Hey, Pop."

His father engulfed him into a hug, slapping his back and

sapping his strength. Whoever said older people were weak had never met Jeremiah Campbell.

"Come on in. Your mother's making her famous lasagna."

Micah's stomach growled. "Garlic bread, too?"

"You know it." His pop chuckled and headed for the galley kitchen.

The kitchen had a peek-a-boo cut out, allowing the cook to see into the living room and the stunning views the marina had to offer. Although he wished his parents were still close by in Bethesda, he had to admit Annapolis had an appeal. The waterfront view seemed to soothe his soul.

"Micah!" his mother called out. She placed her apron on a hook and came from the kitchen, wrapping him in a hug.

"Hi, Mom." He inhaled the scent of butterscotch that always seemed to linger around her. Growing up, his friends always knew she carried a piece of the candy.

"How are you?" she asked, as she pulled back.

"Good. Work is great. Maple Run is a nice place to live." He shrugged.

"Any young ladies catch your eye, Micah?" Her eyebrows rose in one accord.

He suppressed a smile, remembering Belle's frustration at not being able to arch a single eyebrow. "It's complicated."

"Oh, boy. Sounds like a Facebook status." His mom patted the sofa. "Come sit down and tell us all about it."

His stomach growled.

"Food will be ready in a few minutes, but you can have a piece of butterscotch if you want." She pulled the candy out from her pocket.

"No thanks, Mom."

His parents stared at him expectantly. His father had his hands folded over his stomach, his feet raised up on the recliner.

"Oh, you want me to tell you right now."

"Don't play foolish, Micah Campbell." The maternal tone of his mother's voice sent his mind back to his childhood. She had used the same tone whenever he got in trouble.

"Yes, ma'am."

"Who is she?"

"Her name is Belle—"

"Oh, that's the girl your father mentioned." She wagged a finger. "He wouldn't tell me anything past her name."

Micah stared at his dad, who winked at him.

"I told you he'd tell you when he was ready." His father held out a hand toward him. "And look what he's doing…telling you."

"Hush, ol' man," his mom waved a hand in the air as if to say whatever.

"Women," his father muttered.

"Anyway," Micah uttered, trying to hold his laughter back. His parents cracked him up. "Belle's been married before and has a lot of baggage. She thinks she's not good enough for me. But, Mom," he turned toward his father. "Pop, if you met her, you'd like her just as much as I do."

"Then what are you doing about it, dear?" His mother asked. Her leg jiggled impatiently.

"Being patient." *Even though it's killing me.* "I made a promise to be a friend first."

"Hmm," his father murmured. "That's a first for you, son."

"It's what God's calling me to do." Despite his many pleas for the Lord to speed the process up. "And didn't you tell me to listen to Him?"

"Wise beyond my years, I am." His pop waggled his eyebrows as he brought his arms up behind his head.

"Then I suppose that's what you need to do," his mom replied. "Can we at least meet her? Maybe you can bring her to Christmas dinner as a friend?"

"Actually, Mrs. Williams is having a big gathering at her house. She told me to invite you."

"That's nice of her." His mother tilted her head to the side. Her light brown hair didn't move out of its up do.

How many bottles of hairspray froze her hair in place?

"Is your girl going?"

"She's just a friend, Mom." He shrugged. "And I'm not sure."

"Well, try and get her to come, and we'll definitely be there."

"Don't rush me to the altar, Mom." Heat climbed his neck. His mother had been itching for grandchildren for years now. Came from getting old, he guessed.

"Micah Campbell, really? You need a good woman in your life. One better than Denise."

"I'm not disagreeing with you, but I'm not rushing into anything either."

"Have you forgiven Denise?"

Micah turned toward his father, at his question. Had he? Part of him still felt a certain bitterness whenever her name came up. Okay, maybe a lot more than he wanted to admit. "I'm not sure."

His father laid a hand on his shoulder. "I think you need to deal with that before you enter a relationship."

How was he supposed to do that? He'd pledged his life to Denise, and what had she done: betray him. With his cousin! "Pop, I'm not sure that's something that can be easily forgiven."

"It won't be easy, but it's necessary."

"It may be why God is telling you to be patient," his mother added. "God must know you both need work before you enter into a serious relationship."

"True." He couldn't argue with them, even if he wanted to. It was evident he needed to lay his bitterness aside before he could be the man Belle deserved. "I'll try." He sighed.

"Don't try, son," his Pop stated. "Pray and let it go." His father made a hand gesture as if to wash his hands of the whole matter.

"All right, Pop. I'll pray and let it go." Hopefully, it would be as easy as his father made it seem. The Lord knew he was tired of tiptoeing around his cousin at family gatherings.

As his mother got up to check on the food, he headed for their patio for a moment of reflection. He'd pushed his relationship with Denise to the far recesses of his mind, and never bothered to examine it, unless he was around family or someone brought up marriage. Now, he needed to face it head on and completely eradicate the hurt from his life.

*Is that even possible, Lord? Is it really as simple as praying and letting it go? You know I'm tired of this hanging over my head. I want to be the man Belle deserves, and I truly have no idea how my past marriage would affect a future relationship.*

Because he had avoided dating like the plague. If that wasn't evidence of his bitterness, he didn't know what was.

*I'm sorry for hanging onto this longer than necessary. Help me take the necessary steps to forgive her Lord, truly forgive her. And I want to forgive Reggie as well.*

Micah sighed as the prayer left his mind and drifted upward. He needed to let the hurt go. It was past time. Besides, as far as he knew, only he remained hurt and bitter. Reggie and Denise had moved on, and he wanted to be able to as well.

"I forgive them," he whispered.

The words were bitter in his mouth, a testament to the unforgiveness in his heart. Now that he said them, he needed to put action to his declaration.

## 12

Ms. Mable's gift beckoned her. It sat on the dark-brown granite countertop of the kitchen, mocking her fears. Taunting her with the idea that she could create beauty. Instead of giving in, Belle read Proverbs 31. The words describing the mystery woman spoke to the matters of her own heart. Was it truly okay to adorn herself with pretty things? It seemed counterproductive to her walk as a Christian.

Ridding herself of ultra-feminine clothing, makeup, and jewelry had helped her grow close to the Lord. At least that's what she'd thought when she made the choice. It ensured nothing stood in her way to get to know Him and the plans He had for her. The time allowed her to see the quiet beauty in her features, instead of the sensuality that had been present when in flirt mode. Even though Garrett had encouraged her behavior "for the good of sealing a business deal," it didn't remove her culpability. Her actions had been wrong, and she could admit it now. That awful night she took it further...

Well, the scars were a permanent reminder of her sin. Belle was so afraid that outer adornments would open a door and allow sin to come back in her life. She wanted to remain a new creation.

But how did she do that? Besides attempting to erase everything in her past and read her Bible, she wasn't sure of her next steps. Had she gone too far with her outer appearance?

*How do I reconcile between too much and too little, Lord?*

The skirt from the mall hung in her closet, still wrapped in the plastic garment bag the boutique placed it in. She couldn't bring herself to remove it from her closet. The receipt was still in her wallet just in case. Was she making a mistake, imagining herself wearing it to the Christmas Festival and dancing with Micah?

*Yes!*

Okay, so a relationship between her and Micah was a farfetched dream, but still one that pressed upon her heart. The thought of dating him allured her *and* seemed daunting all in one breath. He didn't seem cruel, but neither had Garrett.

*Hindsight, Belle.*

Sure, Garrett had been rude oftentimes, but she had never imagined him as an abuser. How could she be certain Micah wouldn't change too?

*Because he's kind.*

He was so courteous to Mimi and any other woman he came into contact with. And the way he interacted with patients raised her admiration of him. Something told her he would treat her right. Unless, he found out how her marriage ended. Why it ended.

There was no way he'd want to be with an adulterous woman. As awful as Garrett had been to her, he didn't deserve her betrayal. *But he pushed you into it!*

She shook her head at the conflicting thoughts. Garrett told her to ensure the man would sign the deal, not sleep with him. The image of his face when he caught them...a shudder wracked her frame. Garrett had flown into a fit of rage that firmly lodged terror in her heart. When she awoke, she'd laid in the hospital, black and blue. Her wrist had to be pieced together with metal.

Her spleen had been removed and ribs were fractured. Moving had been akin to torture.

All she could do was lay there in that hospital bed and cry. Then Cara, her nurse, shared a Scripture that got her through tough times. *"In my distress I called upon the Lord, and cried unto my God: He heard my voice out of His temple, and my cry came before Him, even into His ears."*

The soft sound of Cara's southern accent filled her mind. She had lain there, full of despair, but the thought of a God that would hear her cry, stilled her tears. Goosebumps raised upon her arms as she remembered feeling the small glimmer of hope that Someone out there truly cared for her. Truly loved her. It wasn't dependent on what she could do for them, but One who desired to listen to her fears, her worries, and her distress.

After that, Cara had held a mini Bible study every day in her room. She even came in on her days off to share the precious words that were a balm to her own aching soul. In that room, Belle had dedicated her life to Christ. The visual of being washed clean and being renewed brought tears to her eyes even now.

*Thank You God, for cleaning me. For not giving up on me. For hearing my cry and picking me up out of the pit of my own doing.*

It was something she prayed she would never forgot. Her actions had led her down an unrighteous path. Of course, she could lay the blame on someone else, but what good would that do? It was what it was, and shirking responsibility wouldn't make it any less than that. Thankfully, God still forgave her.

Overwhelming gratitude rose up, and she bowed her head in prayer. She didn't know what the future held. Didn't know if she would ever marry again or surround herself with things of beauty. But right now, none of that mattered, just the saving grace of a God who loved her beyond compare.

*Thank You for Your love, Heavenly Father. May I never forget the power of it.*

Belle turned and stared at the gift from Ms. Mable. *Lord, I'd like to thank her for thinking of me. Do I have Your permission to make her jewelry?*

She couldn't feel a response in her soul.

What should she do when she didn't hear or feel an answer? She thought of how she bought the dress. Wearing it had felt good. Really good. Feelings of vanity didn't sweep over her, only a quiet acceptance of her appearance. So, she had bought it. Yet, she still didn't know if she should wear it. Maybe it would be the same way with the jewelry. She would take a chance and make something for Ms. Mable. Surely, the words of Proverbs were confirmation it was okay to make something and give it to another?

"Why is life so hard?" Her words echoed in the quiet as the pulse in her temple picked up speed.

Making a decision, she stood and grabbed the gift bag, ridding it of its contents. She would just make a bracelet. Something simple. Nothing extravagant. *I hope.*

"You can do this," Micah said.

He gripped the steering wheel, willing himself to let go and get out of his vehicle. Only, he couldn't. The shine of his good idea had lost all luster. There was no way he wanted to get out of the car and knock on his cousin's door. He glanced to his right, looking out the passenger side window and at Reggie's townhome.

The red brick gleamed in the daylight, the wreath on the door creating a warm welcome. Surprisingly, the home seemed to be decorated in the holiday spirit. Lights lined the townhome and stairway up to the front door. A "Joy to the World" light sign sat in the front yard, waiting for darkness to descend, so it could shine.

Micah never imagined Reggie or Denise as the decorating type. Had he really known them? Before the thought could sink in, the front door opened. His ex-wife filled the doorway, arms folded across her chest, probably due to the chill in the air. Now, he had no choice but to exit his SUV.

"Please help me, Lord." He got out and headed up the walkway to the stairs. *Forgive, Campbell, forgive.* He took the steps, one at a time, his mind repeating the litany.

Denise looked at him, wariness darkening her features. Her brow scrunched further as he stopped on the landing. "Micah?"

The question in her voice was unmistakable. Considering he told her he never wanted to speak to them again, he understood her confusion. He slid his hands into his coat pockets. "Hello, Denise."

She looked over her shoulder, then at him. "Do you...do you want to come in?"

He nodded, too nervous to speak any further.

Denise backed away from the door, clutching her sweater tight as he passed her. "Reggie is in the basement. Should I call him up?" The words held a tremor.

Was she as nervous as he? "Um, I'd like to speak to you first."

She gestured to the living room behind him. He quickly sat down on the couch, sliding his hands along his pants leg. "I wanted to say..." He paused. *Just say you forgive her. Say it and let the pain go.*

"Look, before you go on, I need to tell you something." She looked up at the ceiling.

He nodded, taking the reprieve she offered.

"I'm sorry," she rushed out, meeting his gaze. "What I did was inexcusable and unforgivable. Not only did I betray your trust, but I caused a rift in your family." A tear slipped down her cheek. "Please forgive me."

*This.*

This is what he'd wanted when he first discovered them. An honest apology and a plea of forgiveness. He'd imagined laughing in her face over and over. Of shutting the door in her face and wiping contrition from his cousin's face with his fist. Yet, now that they were in this moment, all he wanted was to be done with the whole thing. He couldn't take the bitterness anymore. Avoiding family, so that he didn't have to hear about them, had grown tiresome.

"I forgive you." The words flew free and a weight lifted from his body. He sagged into the couch, overcome. "I forgive you," he said again.

"Really?" She wiped her face. "How can you? You were so angry..."

"I'm tired of being angry. I can't live like this the rest of my life. I need to let this go."

Surprise lifted her eyebrows.

"Denise!" Reggie called out.

Micah turned and saw his cousin jogging up the stairs.

When Reggie saw him, he froze. "What are you doing here, cuz?" Reggie glanced at his wife then back at Micah. "What did you say to her?"

"Calm down, babe." Denise stood up, going to his side. "I was just apologizing to Micah." She wiped an errant tear. "It's all right." She placed a hand on his chest as if to stay him. "It's all right."

Micah stared at his cousin. The one who had been more like a brother. "I just came to apologize, Reg. That's all."

Reggie's jaw tensed. His cousin looked him up and down, judging him.

Had this been a month ago, Micah would have been tempted to spew venom with his words. Strangely, calm and peace filled him. He knew it could only have been a blessing from the Lord. "I'm sorry I widened the divide between us. You tried to apologize, and I never gave you a chance. I'm sorry."

Reggie's shoulders sagged. "No. I can't say that you were in the wrong for acting like that. What I did...what we did..." Reggie sighed and stepped forward. "I'm sorry, too. I should have told you how I felt. I know it probably wouldn't have made a difference since you were married, but..." Reggie shrugged and then offered a hand, "truce?"

"Truce." He shook his hand.

After a few minutes, Micah left their house with a clear conscience. As he drove back home, he thought about how defensive Reggie had been. Their rift had gone on so long, each felt their behavior was right, considering the grievances. *How exhausting.* He ran a hand over his head.

*Lord, thank You for showing me the error of my ways. I pray that I can truly let forgiveness rule in my heart and don't pick the hurt back up again. I pray that the awkwardness will slowly fade over time.*

"Amen," he whispered.

## 13

"Belle, want to go to The Pit for lunch?" Micah looked at her expectantly as she came to a stop in the hallway.

The way he stared at her...well, it made her wonder if he had something other than lunch on his mind. Not in a nefarious way, but the kind that elicited goosebumps up her arms and across her nape, making her heart skip a beat. Too bad he didn't know she was bad news.

*So, tell him.*

"Um, I'm going to the Crafting Corner at lunch time." Okay, so she went with the avoidance method, but she just wasn't strong enough to say no out right.

"Will you be there long? I can wait for you? Save you a seat at the bar?"

Her stomach dipped. Why did he have to make it so difficult?

*It's just lunch, Belle.*

But she wanted so much more. "Um, I'm not sure how long it will take."

"I can wait."

Belle stared at him. He was always willing to wait. And hadn't she agreed to be friends? "Okay, sure. You can save me a seat."

A grin lit up his face, chasing the uncertainty away that her hesitancy had caused. "Great, see you at lunch." He walked away, a low whistle trailing in his wake.

She continued down the hall toward the front office. She needed to call the next patient. The chart in her hand belonged to a little girl, but all she could think about was Micah's grin and the warmth in his eyes. *Lord, please help me to not fall for him. He deserves so much better than me.*

The rest of the time rushed by quickly and lunch time was ushered in on the sound of Mariah Carey's pipes as she sang about Christmas. Belle left the family practice and headed over to Ms. Mable's craft store. She should have stopped by sooner to thank her for the gift. Even if the gift had caused her to run for some antacids. All she needed to do was walk in there, say "thank you," and give Ms. Mable the bracelet she had made last night.

*What a way to start a Monday.*

Belle had used green and brown stones to make the achingly gorgeous bracelet. It reminded her of the beautiful trees that lined the Virginia skyline. And the part of her that still longed for beauty in all its avenues couldn't help but imagine it with the skirt she bought. Which is why she was giving it to Ms. Mable.

Jewelry making turned out to be fun and had kept her entertained for hours, but she couldn't keep her creations at her place. Looked like her friends would be getting matching jewelry to go with the scarves she crocheted for Christmas gifts. She shook her head, chuckling to herself. Never in a million years would she have imagined giving people homemade gifts.

Garrett would have been livid if she had made him a gift instead of adding to his repertoire of high-priced possessions. Probably would have jostled her or slapped her around to express his extreme displeasure. Her brow furrowed at a similar memory.

"Belle, get in here!"

*Oh, no!* She dropped the magazine and rushed into the bathroom. "I can explain, Garrett."

His hand snaked out and grabbed her around the throat. Her heartbeat skyrocketed as she struggled to breathe.

"I told you I wanted a fresh towel waiting for me every day. Why is that so hard for you to understand?"

Tears welled in her eyes and she pushed at his hands. He shoved her away, disgust twisting the features on his dark skin. "I can't imagine why your mama thought you'd be a good wife. Too busy looking at magazines and worrying about your appearance." The whole time he talked, he unbuttoned his cuff links, working his sleeves up his forearms.

Fear gripped her mind, froze her in its tentacles, as she lay on the floor, gasping for sweet, precious air. She knew she should apologize again, but her heart stumbled at a rapid pace as it welcomed the oxygen into her blood stream. Whenever he raised his sleeves, she knew it was only a matter of time before he decided to get physical. She swallowed, wincing at the tenderness.

"Garrett, the washer is broken," she rasped out. "I called the repairman, but he couldn't come out today." She stared at the carpet, refusing to meet his gaze, but hoping he took it for contrition.

Would he accept her words or punish her for things that were beyond her control?

"Who did you call?" Steel lined his words, as his feet came into her peripheral vision.

"Manuel."

Silence met her ears for a heartbeat. Then another. And another.

"Manuel, it's Garrett Peterson."

Sounds of the handyman's voice reached her ears, but she couldn't make out the words.

"When did she call you? And you still can't make it?"

Belle slowly lifted her eyes and stopped as she realized Garrett watched her.

"Fine. She'll be here."

He ended the call. "Manuel says you called first thing this morning."

She nodded, too afraid to do anything else.

"Why didn't you go buy some fresh ones?"

"They were too expensive. I didn't have enough money." His taste in towels was as expensive as his taste in clothing. Since he had her on an allowance, it wasn't enough to cover the added amount. Plus, he forbade her to call him while working.

Paper fell into her vision. Slowly, she reached for the hundred-dollar bill.

"I'll wait. I expect you to be quick about it."

Tears fell from her eyes as the memory faded. She praised God every day for keeping her location hidden from her ex-husband. She never wanted to see him again. Belle wiped her face as she pulled into Mable's Crafting Corner. *Get your act together, Belle.* A quick glance in the visor mirror confirmed her eyes weren't as red as she thought they'd be. She grabbed the gift box from the passenger seat and headed inside.

"Good afternoon, Belle."

"Hi, Ms. Mable."

The portly woman came from behind the cash register. "Do you need help with something?"

"Actually, I brought you something." She held out the gift box.

"For me? Really?" Ms. Mable beamed as she took the gift. She opened the box and sighed. "Belle, I knew you'd do a wonderful job. This is gorgeous." She slipped the bracelet on. "Thank you so much."

Before Belle knew what was happening, the older woman enveloped her in a hug. Tears sprang to her eyes as Ms. Mable squeezed her tight. When was the last time she had a hug?

"You're such a sweetheart." Ms. Mable pulled back, laying a hand on her heart.

Belle offered a tremulous smile. "I wanted to thank you. Sorry, I haven't been by sooner."

"Oh, nonsense." Ms. Mable waved a hand. "I'm just glad you liked the jewelry set. I wasn't sure if you would or not."

"Well..." she faltered, wondering how to make her understand the conflict going on inside. "Ms. Mable, I'm just not so sure I should be wearing it." She slid her hands into her coat pockets to hide the tremors in her hands.

"Why ever not, dear?"

"Isn't that vanity?"

"So, you made a bracelet for me, causing me to stumble over the vanity block?"

"Oh, no." Horror struck her heart. "I didn't mean to do that at all."

"Oh, Belle." Ms. Mable engulfed her hand between hers. "Sweetie, whatever is going on inside, you need to turn that over to God. You can't continue to beat yourself up for something that happened in the past. Something that I'm *sure* God has forgiven you for, because judging from that scared expression, you've asked forgiveness repeatedly."

"I need to make sure He understands how sorry I am, Ms. Mable."

"Honey, He heard your prayer the first time you uttered it. Forgave it the moment He saw the remorse in your heart." Ms. Mable pointed toward the organ in question. "That might as well be on your sleeve the way you're carrying on. He believed you the first time, so why are you living like you're unforgiven?"

The tears were back, but this time she couldn't prevent them from spilling over. "I just don't want to go back to a life of sin."

"Then don't, dear heart. Wearing jewelry doesn't cause one to sin. It's what's in the heart."

Belle sniffed, trying to stop the tears. "But you just said we could have stumbling blocks."

"Of course, you can. Everyone has a trigger, a temptation, but don't forget the good Lord provides an escape from it. You don't have to go down that path if you don't want. He always makes a way."

"I don't want to."

"Then keep your eyes on Him, Belle. He's the Creator and He's given you a gift of creating. To bring joy to others. To shine the beauty of light into someone's darkness. Seek Him first in everything and He'll help you avoid the sin of vanity. If I were a betting woman, I'd take a gamble that you've had a heart change, and that's what matters the most. Not the outward trappings, what's inside."

"Oh, Ms. Mable." This time she wrapped her arms around the wise woman of God.

"It's okay." She patted her head. "God's got you, sweetie."

The truth of her words fell softly like fresh rain against her battered heart, as her tears slowly came to a stop. Her heart had changed. Beauty and its friends no longer ruled inside, but her Heavenly Father did.

And she needed to remember that.

☙

The bell tinkled, signaling a newcomer. Micah swiveled around, checking to see if Belle had entered. He sighed. Where was she? He'd been waiting for...he glanced at his watch. Fifteen minutes. He purposely left five minutes after she had. What was taking her so long?

The chime sounded again. Did he dare turnaround? He wasn't used to the needy feeling that coursed through him with just the thought of her. When had the desire to be her friend morphed into more? It was almost laughable, except he ached knowing that God had told him that he still needed to wait. Patience would be the death of him.

*I hate to sound ungrateful and whiny, but how much longer, Lord?*

"Hey, sorry I'm late."

He looked up, surprised to see Belle standing next to him. Her eyes looked red as if she'd been crying. "Hey."

She smiled and slipped onto the seat. "Did you order already?"

"Just a drink." *Why were you crying?* The question begged to be asked, but he didn't want to overstep the line. Just how much could a patient friend—okay, hardly patient—ask before he entered the none-of-your-business arena?

"Sorry it took me so long. I had a nice talk with Ms. Mable and kind of lost track of the time."

"Oh, good." *The kind that makes you cry? How is that good?* "How is she?"

"Good. I brought her a bracelet I made as a thank you for all she's done."

He nodded, wondering when he could break the mindless chit chat and get down to the real story. But before he could ask, Dee walked over.

"Hey girl. You want the usual?"

"Yes, please," Belle said.

"Micah, you?"

"Um, sure."

Belle turned to him, a quizzical expression on her face. "You okay?"

"Actually, I was wondering the same thing about you." He grabbed the straw casing to keep his hands from touching her face. "You look like you've been crying." *Smooth, Campbell.*

Belle bit her lip. "That obvious?"

"No, you're still beautiful. Just a touch of sadness in your eyes."

Her mouth parted in surprise. "You think I'm beautiful? I'm not even wearing makeup."

He chuckled, couldn't help it. She looked so stunned. "Belle, you don't need makeup to be beautiful. You have a natural beauty that shines as bright as your heart."

"Micah Campbell, you surprise me every single time I'm with you."

"Is that a good thing?" *Please say it is.*

"Maybe." She quirked a half grin his way. "Want to hear a joke?"

"Sure."

"What did Potassium think of his date with Oxygen?"

He quirked an eyebrow. Another one of her weird chemistry jokes. "What?"

"It was OK." She laughed, snorting.

Micah couldn't help but join in. "Okay, that was bad."

"Ok?" She laughed again.

"Girl, you're a trip."

Delaney came back and sat their drinks in front of them. She leaned against the counter. "Are you two going to the Christmas festival?" Something passed in her eyes as she stared at Belle, but he couldn't be sure what.

"I'm going." He looked at Belle. "You?" *Please go, please go.* If she went, maybe it could turn into a date preview, or something to that effect.

"I haven't decided." She stared back at Delaney, but he couldn't read her eyes.

Something was going on, but what? "You and Luke going?"

"We are. It's just so happens the festival falls on date night."

"Date night?" Belle asked.

"Since I have two kids, dates aren't that plentiful. But we try and go out every other Friday. Plus, his job keeps him busy."

"Jumping's in his blood," he said.

"Tell me about it." Delaney smiled. "Your food will be right out." She walked away.

"What does that mean? Jumping's in his blood."

"Oh, Delaney didn't tell you the story?"

"No," Belle swiveled a little on the bar stool to look at him fully.

"Luke used to jump out of planes when he was in the Army. Now, he takes people up for skydiving lessons."

A shudder racked her frame and she grimaced. "That's insane."

"Nah, it's fun."

"You've done it?"

"Of course. You want to try?" Her eyes widened, and a burst of laughter flew from his lips. "I take it that's a no."

"Definitely."

"How about this, you go to the Christmas festival, and I'll table the skydiving conversation for a little while, *friend*." He wasn't sure why he needled her, but he couldn't take the words back.

"Easy choice. See you at the festival."

## 14

Why on earth did she agree to go to the Christmas party? Belle stared at her closet, the skirt calling out toward her. It wouldn't be considered a Christmas outfit, but it had pockets and twirl factor. Obviously, she'd wear it considering the dress-up aspect.

She lightly tapped her forehead at her stupidity. If she didn't know better, she'd think Micah taunted her on purpose to get her to go to the festival. Didn't he hear her say she was no good?

*Lord, why did this week fly by so fast?*

Christmas was in two days and the festival started at seven tonight. Fortunately, Delaney had invited her over for Christmas and apparently Micah too. There was nowhere she could go to avoid the man. And boy, was she trying. Her eyes closed on their own accord as she remembered his woodsy scent. Every time they ate at The Pit, it seemed to surround her. Instead of enjoying the delicious maple-cooked foods, her nose seemed intent to take in Micah's cologne.

And his smile! It lit up his whole face. She could only imagine what he must have looked like as a child. His mom probably gave into his every whim.

*Like you are?*

She rolled her eyes as she got dressed, muttering about the impossibilities of good-looking men. Well, not all men, but Micah. He turned her inside out. Had her wishing for things that just weren't a possibility for her anymore. She was damaged goods and would do well to remember that. Her focus needed to remain solely on the Lord.

But tonight, she would try and have fun. No sense getting dressed and hanging with friends if she didn't at least make an attempt to have fun. Hopefully, one of the girls would keep her company and run interference in case Micah came around.

*But they're married!*

Delaney wasn't, but close enough. And Nikki, she remained single. Maybe she'd beg Nikki to be a wallflower. Although, her friend had sounded like she thought dancing sounded like fun.

Could she dance with Micah? Would she?

Sighing, she grabbed the strappy heels she splurged on. Thankfully, they were closed toed, so she didn't have to worry about a lack of nail polish. Instead, she wiped a plum lip gloss on her lips, combed her hair to a shine, and twirled it a couple of times just for fun.

Belle grinned. Now that that was out of her, she could go to the festival.

The town hall gleamed in its Christmas splendor. Lights framed the building as sounds of the season leaked outdoors from the speakers. Belle smiled at Dr. Kerrington, who held the door open.

"Merry Christmas," he said.

"Merry Christmas, Dr. K."

"You make sure to have fun in there, Belle. You deserve it for all the hard work you do."

*Aw. Dr. K was such a sweet man. "Thank you."* With a goodbye she walked in, scanning the premises for the girls.

Right away, she spotted Delaney and Luke on the dance floor. They were wrapped up in each other's arms, foreheads touching. Romance practically dripped from them. Delaney looked gorgeous in a red maxi dress, which matched Luke's plaid-button down shirt.

She never matched with a man, but it sounded so romantic. *Don't fall into the trap, Belle. Find Nikki and persevere!* Once again, she searched and instead found Nina and Dwight.

*Come on, Lord! The romance is killing me.*

"Hey, girl," Nikki said.

Belle whirled around, relief pouring over her.

"Did you just get here?"

"I did. I was looking for you."

Nikki beamed, her auburn hair falling down to her shoulders. She looked stunning in a navy blue, lace dress. "Well, you found me." Nikki looked her up and down, then squeezed her arm. "I'm so glad you wore the skirt."

Belle forced a smile. "Nothing else to wear."

"Oh, Belle, you're going to have fun. Trust me."

"All right," she sighed. "I will."

"Great, then let's go check your coat and grab some food."

The tables were lined up in a single line and filled buffet style. Smells of fried chicken, baked mac-n-cheese, and other deliciousness wafted toward her. "Did Mrs. Williams and Dwight cater this?"

"Of course," Nikki said with a smile. "I skipped the main meal and had a slice of the maple bacon cheesecake when I got here."

"My kind of girl, dessert first."

"Definitely."

They chatted quietly as they filled their plates and then headed for the seating area, which lined the perimeter of the dance floor.

"Did you see Nina and Delaney?"

"They were on the dance floor when I got here," Belle replied. "Aren't they just adorable?"

*Disgustingly so.* Belle blinked, surprised by the bitterness which had risen up. Since when did she begrudge anyone happiness?

"Belle, you okay?"

"Yeah, just having a minor meltdown."

"Jealous?" Nikki asked, her mouth twisting.

"Surprisingly so."

"We've all been there."

"Really? What do you have to be jealous about?" She stared at her new friend. Nikki always seemed happy and full of cheer. She would have never pictured her as the envious sort.

"Sometimes I want what they have."

"Then what's stopping you?"

"Can't shake the demons from the past."

Her curiosity meter shot up. What had happened to make her friend so morose? "Do you want to talk about it?"

Nikki shook her head. "Not today. Today, I'm going to remember that God loves me, and I have friends and yeah…that's that."

"Well, if you ever change your mind, I'm sure there'll be men lining up."

Nikki scoffed. "Not likely."

"Then why has Shorty been staring at you since we sat down?" For a moment, she thought he'd been looking at her, but he never made eye contact. It didn't take a high IQ to figure out who had captured his attention.

Nikki's cheeks flamed bright as she glanced his way. "Shorty and I are friends."

"Girl, friends don't look at one another like that."

"That's how Micah looks at you."

Her mouth dropped open. She closed it as her heart galloped in her chest at the thought. Did he really look at her like that? A spark of some unknown emotion flickered inside. "Micah and I are just friends."

"Aren't we a pair?"

※

Music drew Micah in as he opened the door to the town hall. He purposely showed up thirty minutes late, so he wouldn't be tempted to walk right up to Belle. Because the sad thing was, he had been dressed and ready to go thirty minutes prior to the party. But first, he needed to grab some food. He'd been looking forward to the maple-fried chicken all day long.

Hopefully, showing up late didn't mean he'd have slim pickings. He headed toward the buffet and pulled up short. Shorty twirled Belle around on the dance floor. Her cheeks were flushed, and a wide smile graced her beautiful face.

*She's gorgeous.*

He couldn't believe it. He'd never seen her wear a dress or skirt before. The tan blouse showed her curves and remained tucked into a skirt full of colors. They merged like a kaleidoscope as Shorty twirled her once more. As she came to a stop, her skirt stilled, showing the different colors.

Before he realized it, his feet had propelled him forward. He slowed as they turned toward him.

"Micah, my man, how's it going?" Shorty bumped his fist.

"Good, just got here."

"You're missing all the fun!" Belle's eyes shined bright, the mahogany color dazzling him.

"Want to help me catch up?" His mouth tilted in what he hoped resembled a smile, but his pulse was too erratic to ensure it.

"Hey, man," Shorty said. "Why don't you dance with Belle? I'm going to see if Nikki wants to dance."

Belle looked at him expectantly.

"Can I have this dance?"

She nodded, placing a hand in his. He dropped his hands to her waist as the music slowed into "White Christmas." Electricity charged the air as his eyes locked onto hers. He wanted to tell her how beautiful she was, but the words were stuck in his throat. Her skin radiated warmth against his palms.

*Lord, help me out here! I'm about to cave in.*

"Have you eaten yet?" Belle asked, her words a little husky.

"No, saw you and wanted to say hi." *Couldn't help but say hi.*

"Shorty's been dancing since he walked in." Belle glanced over her shoulder, her eyes widening.

He turned and saw Nikki and Shorty dancing as well. "Never thought I'd see that."

"No kidding. She seems to avoid him at length, but there's an undercurrent there."

"Like the one between us." Micah squeezed his eyes shut. He hadn't meant to say that aloud.

"Micah, you know why we can't."

He met her gaze, frowning at the look of sadness in her eyes. "Is it because we work together?"

"No, but you have to admit that's a point for the con column."

He felt his eyebrow arch. "You've been making a pros-and-cons list?"

"Uh..." her cheeks flushed. "I'm just saying that if something went wrong, work would become awkward."

"Or nothing will go wrong."

She sighed, and the cool air caressed his skin. He drew her closer, his eyes dropping to her lips.

"Don't look at me like that," she breathed out.

"I can't help it."

He dipped his head. Belle's eyes widened. She jerked back, and her hands flew to her face. Were they rosy or had they paled in annoyance? He wanted to groan in frustration as cold replaced the warmth of her. "Belle, I'm sorry."

"No, it's fine. I...I'm going to go find Nikki." She whirled around and left him standing on the dance floor.

Micah rubbed his chin. Frustration crashed against him like waves on a rock. Why couldn't he remember to be a friend? He blinked as Luke walked up to him.

"What was that about?" Luke tilted his head in Belle's departing direction.

"Got too close."

"Huh, I thought you would have asked her out by now."

"God seems to want me to wait, but I keep messing up."

"Don't we all."

Luke clapped him on the shoulder. "Don't worry, Soup. She'll come around."

"Not if I push her away."

"Just don't dance with her and you'll be right as rain." Luke chuckled and wondered off, probably to find Delaney.

Micah headed toward the buffet table. This time he'd get his chicken and avoid Belle, give her a chance to cool down. He snorted. Who was he kidding? *He* needed a chance to cool down.

Fortunately, the buffet still had food. He smiled in greeting when he spotted Mrs. Williams filling a container with fresh food.

"Why aren't you dancing, Micah?"

"I was, but the smell of your chicken brought me to my senses."

She laughed. "Laying it on a lil' thick, aren't you?"

"Are you kidding? I love your chicken."

She dipped her head in acknowledgment. "Have you danced with Belle yet?" Curiosity brightened her face.

Mrs. Williams didn't look her age at all. Her hair fell to her shoulder in soft waves. There were no visible wrinkles, and the makeup she wore only enhanced her looks. He could tell Delaney would age the same way. "Why don't you go dance and enjoy yourself? I'm sure Dwight could man the table."

Her eyes widened. "There aren't a lot of people my age to dance with." She stepped back.

She appeared uneasy, and for some reason that tickled him. Most of the time, he was on the other end of the conversation. With a grin, he scanned the crowd looking for someone her age and unattached.

"What about Mr. Norton?" Micah pointed to the gentleman, who had just entered the front door. "I'm sure he needs a break from greeting everyone."

"Well..." she sputtered trying to think of something to say.

"You know what, Mrs. Williams? I'll go get him." He strolled away whistling. Perhaps Mr. Norton could occupy her long enough for her to stay out of everyone's business.

After speaking to Mr. Norton, the older man shook his hand and headed towards Mrs. Williams.

Luke walked up to him. "What are you up to, Soup?"

"Got Mrs. Williams a dance partner."

A bark of laughter tore from Luke. "Oh, I gotta tell Delaney." Luke looked around and found his fiancée and waved her over.

"What's up?" She hooked an arm around Luke then turned toward Micah. "Merry Christmas, Soup."

"Merry Christmas, Dee." He nodded toward Mrs. Williams. "Found your mother a dance partner."

Delaney's eyes grew wide as saucers. "Bless your heart. I never thought of setting her up with someone."

"Genius, isn't it?" Luke asked.

"Oh, Dwight's going to love this." She scanned the crowds and motioned her brother over.

They exchanged pleasantries and then Dee pointed out their mother. A huge grin split Dwight's face. "Perfect, Micah. Maybe we should set her up. Think she'll stay out of our hair if she does?"

"Couldn't hurt to try," he replied.

Delaney clasped her hands together. "Sounds like we need to sit down and come up with a plan. I'll go get the ladies."

## 15

Belle's phone rang, breaking the silence in her apartment. She glanced at the caller ID and a smile lit her face. *Cara!* She hadn't talked to her friend since she started working, hadn't wanted to be a burden.

"Hi, Cara!"

"Hey, there, Belle. I just wanted to call and wish you a Merry Christmas." The twang in her voice brought a smile to Belle's face.

She put her gifts down and sank into the sofa. Mrs. Williams' Christmas party could wait a little bit. "Merry Christmas to you, too. Are you celebrating with your sister?" Cara's parents had passed suddenly, and she now had custody of her teenager sister.

"I sure am. Becky brought her boyfriend." Her voice dropped. "Not sure how I feel about him yet."

"If anyone can make a person better it'll be you."

"I hope so," she sighed. "How are you celebrating Christ's birth, Belle?"

"I've been invited to a Christmas dinner."

"So, you've made friends?"

*Have I?* She nodded, then realized Cara couldn't see her. "I have." She leaned back and told her about The Pit and all the people she'd met since moving to town.

"Sounds like you like the place."

"I do. Everyone's so nice and they seem to genuinely care."

"I'm so happy. Have you found a church too?"

"Yes, the pastor is very down-to-earth and makes the Bible so easy to understand. I wish you could hear him preach."

"Maybe I'll come visit one day."

Her heart warmed. "I'd love that. I don't have the place in my apartment, it's a one bedroom. But there's a B&B in town and everything is close by."

"Have you had any visitors?"

Belle sighed, "No." She sat up. "But it's okay. I'm making friends. I enjoy my work, and like I said, I have church."

"Have you called your mother, Belle?"

Belle shook her head. Why did Cara always have to bring her up and ruin the conversation. "She doesn't want to hear from me. Don't you remember? Not a single visit for all the time I spent there."

"I'm sure she misses you."

"I'm not and you don't have to come up with some platitude to assuage me. It's okay; it really is." The protest fell from her lips as quickly as one would drop a hot pot. But even she knew she protested too much.

"I'll be praying for y'alls relationship. Maybe you could take a step to restore it."

Like she did in the hospital? *No.* Her mother didn't want to hear from her and she'd leave it like that. "Well, I have to go." Because she no longer wanted to talk about the lack of her mother's presence. "I'm heading to Mrs. Williams' house right now."

"Okay, don't be a stranger. Call me or even text from time to time."

"I will," she said with a smile.

Belle grabbed her gifts and opened the door. She stopped

short, almost missing the wrapped box that sat on her welcome mat. Once again, she placed her gifts down and picked up the one outside her door. Her name had been scrawled on the front as if someone dropped it off rather than have it delivered, which made sense because it was Sunday.

She glanced at her watch. *6:55pm.* If she didn't leave now, she'd be late for dinner. She placed the gift on her countertop and grabbed her homemade ones. *I'll just have to open it later.* But curiosity plagued her all the way to Mrs. Williams' home. Who would have just left something on her doorstep? And, she hadn't heard anyone knock or footfalls going up the stairs.

Her mouth dropped open as she noticed all the cars lined on the driveway of the Williams' property. She assumed that they had only invited family and close friends, but it looked like all the patrons of The Pit had decided to show up.

*Lord, please don't let me stick out like a sore thumb. Help me to have fun. In Jesus' Name, Amen.*

Exhaling her worries away, she grabbed her belongings and walked up the driveway to Mrs. Williams' farmhouse. Lights framed the house and the porch railing. The lights appeared to dance almost to the beat of the music that poured from the house. A chalkboard sign stood on the porch. It read: COME ON IN.

With a smile, she opened the screen door and headed into the fray. Shorty and an older couple were standing in the foyer, laughing and talking. She smiled in greeting as she searched for one of the ladies. She spotted Nikki in the dining room, setting food on the table.

"Merry Christmas, Nikki."

Her friend looked up. "Merry Christmas!" She ran around the side of the table and squeezed Belle in a hug. "I'm so glad you came. Do you need help with that?" she asked, pointing to the gifts.

"No, I got it. Just so happens your gift is on top."

"Aw, thank you, Belle."

Belle glanced back in the foyer. "Who's that with Shorty?"

"His mom and dad." Her mouth twisted. Nikki looked kind of nervous.

What was going on with those two? She'd leave Nikki to her demons and give her a reprieve. "Who else is here?"

"Micah and his parents are here. And of course, Nina, Delaney and their families. Oh, and you get to meet Kandi. She got home last night."

So, maybe it was friends and family only. She wiped her hands against her slacks, trying to steel the nerves. Why did being surrounded by family bother her so? *Maybe because you don't have a family.* She inhaled, stunned by the hurt that speared her heart.

"You okay, Belle?"

"Sure," she nodded. "I'm going to go find Nina and Delaney, so I can give them their gifts." *And try not to cry.*

Maybe Cara had a point. Perhaps it was time to restore her relationship with her mother. But what if she hung up on her again. Abandoned her once more? Shaking off the melancholy thoughts, she headed for the kitchen. Delaney had just walked in from the living room.

"Merry Christmas, Dee."

"Belle! Merry Christmas." Delaney pressed her cheek to hers. "Whatcha got there?"

"Gifts for you and Nina."

"Thanks, girl. I'll put them under the tree." Delaney took the gifts and left before Belle could object.

She stood there feeling lost. Should she help prepare the table?

"Belle?"

She tensed at the sound of Micah's voice. Ever since their dance at the Christmas Festival, she'd felt a little uneasy. Even now, her heart raced forward like a runner sprinting for a gold medal. Turning, she found Micah and his parents looking at her expectantly. *Great.*

Belle looked like the proverbial deer in the headlights. Micah cleared his throat as he gestured toward his parents. "This is my mom, Beverly, and my father, Jeremiah."

Belle offered a hand toward his mother. "Nice to meet you, Mrs. Campbell."

"Oh, please, call me Beverly."

Belle smiled, but it looked forced.

He sighed. *Lord, please don't let her be nervous. It's not like she's "really" meeting my parents. We're all just here to celebrate Your Son.* And maybe he wanted his parents to meet Belle. *Okay, so I'm not fooling You, but I still want her to be less stressed.*

"Mr. Campbell," Belle said, shaking his hand.

"You can call me Jeremiah. Micah told us about his charming coworker."

Belle glanced at him. He offered a reassuring smile. His pop's words sure weren't going to ease her nerves.

"It's nice to meet you. You've raised a good man."

His mother clutched her heart. "Oh, you just made my day. I tell you, we had worries when he was about three years old. They warn you about the terrible twos, but his third year made his second year look like a cake walk." His mother shuddered delicately.

Micah held back laughter. His mother told that story to anyone who'd listen. He wasn't sure how much was truth and how much she exaggerated for effect.

"I can believe it." Belle's eyes lit up with laughter. "He's always teasing the kids at work."

"He got his humor from me," Pop stated.

"Tell him one of your jokes, Belle," Micah stated. He knew Pop would get a kick out of them. They had the same type of humor.

She shook her head. "Oh no, I'm not sure he'll like them."

He turned toward his parents. "Belle likes science jokes."

"This I gotta hear," his mother said.

"Okay," she took a deep breath. "What do you call iron blowing in the wind?"

"What?" his father asked.

She deadpanned, "*Fe*-breeze."

Micah shook his head while his father's deep laughter filled the room. His mom chuckled, but he couldn't be sure if she liked the joke or just the sound of his father's laughter.

"I have more where that came from." Belle's cheeks flushed.

His pop reached out, squeezing her hand. "Might want to spread them out. I can't laugh like that all the time."

"Sure thing, Mr. Campbell."

"Ah uh ah, it's Jeremiah, remember?"

"Yes." She dipped her head but still didn't say his name.

Was it because they were her elders? "Would you like to sit next to us at the table, Belle?" He didn't want her feeling alone.

"Maybe. I was going to ask if Nikki wanted to sit near me. I don't think she has anyone to sit with."

If Shorty had anything to do with it, Nikki would be sitting next to him and his parents. "Just let me know."

"Sure." She smiled at his parents. "It was nice meeting you both."

"Likewise, Belle. Don't be a stranger the rest of the night, okay?" his mother asked.

"Yes, ma'am."

She dipped her head and walked away. Probably thanking her lucky stars she had an out to not sit by them.

"Well, son, I can see why you're smitten."

"Pop."

"What? You can't tell me you aren't. I saw the way you stared at her."

"That's what people do when they're having a conversation. It's rude not to look at someone while they're talking."

"Micah Campbell, you know good and well you don't stare at

everyone like that," his mom chastised. "No harm in admitting you like the girl."

"I just don't want you to make a big deal out of it. I told you there's a past there."

"We know, son," his Pop said, laying a hand on his shoulder. "God's going to work it out. Take a deep breath and calm yourself."

"He's just about as high-strung as you are, Jeremiah Campbell," his mother huffed.

His dad snorted. "He gets that weak constitution from your side, Beverly. We Campbells come from hardy stock. A girl doesn't scare us."

"Hmmm, I'm sure you'll be thinking that from the couch tonight," his mother walked off.

"Now, Beverly..." his father followed, beseeching his mom.

Micah stood there, indecision rooting him in place. Part of him wanted to find Belle and make sure she was okay. He couldn't imagine how she felt being here and not part of a family unit. Granted, her invitation here was to ensure she would not be left out, but still. But if he did find her, would she feel like he was suffocating her? He didn't want to press, just wanted to be a friend.

*Stop making it complicated, Campbell.*

He sighed and turned, scanning the room. She wasn't in the living room. He headed for the dining room and nodded in passing as Shorty and Nikki stood in the foyer. If they were talking, then maybe he still had a chance to sit with Belle for dinner.

Micah found her in the dining room, setting some trays down. "Hey."

"Hi." She smiled and straightened out a tray. "Where are your parents?"

"Probably off somewhere making up." He twisted his mouth. "They like to argue for that purpose."

Belle chuckled. "That's adorable."

"Or nauseating."

"Are you embarrassed?" She tilted the side of her head, studying him.

Suddenly, it felt warm in the room. "Do you want to see your parents kiss?"

Her nose wrinkled. "Okay, maybe you have a point."

"I know I do." He chuckled, moving around the table. He stopped a couple of feet from her. "Will you sit with me? I promise to be on my best behavior."

"Just friends?"

"First and foremost."

## 16

Surprisingly, New Year's came and went by quietly. Since it fell on a Sunday, Dr. Kerrington had the offices closed on Monday in observance. Belle decided to leave her four walls and find some semblance of fun elsewhere.

Hence the reason she sat in one of the booths at The Pit. When it came down to it, there wasn't a lot to do in the winter time in Maple Run. She could have driven to the next town or the mall, but none of that appealed to her. So, she sat at the booth wishing she had chosen the bar instead.

*Why didn't you?*

She shrugged inwardly while her thoughts swirled around. She'd been feeling melancholy ever since Christmas dinner. Even though she'd joked and laughed with Micah, loneliness and sadness had still pressed upon her. He kept dropping hints that he wanted to be more than friends, but she just didn't think she could handle it. As much as she wanted to grasp the hand he offered, fear prevented her.

What if he found out about her past? Realized how short she measured up? She'd be crushed. *And that's different than now, how?*

"I don't know," she whispered.

"Hey, girl," Nina stated.

Belle looked up, meeting her gaze. "Hey, Nina. How are you?"

"Tired," she huffed. She pointed toward the empty side of the booth. "Can I sit?"

"Of course!"

Nina shuffled into the booth, rubbing her round belly. "You looked kind of sad, so I wanted to say hi."

"Pretty much sums it up."

"What's going on?"

She shrugged. Sure, she'd told Nina about her past, but how could she tell her about the dreams of her future. To give them voice made them seem more precious. "Just thinking."

"Care to share?" Nina held up her hands. "You don't have to."

"I was just wondering how you know when to give someone a chance."

"You talking about Micah?"

Belle nodded.

"Are we ever a hundred percent sure of anything? At least when it comes to our thoughts and choices?"

"Not often."

"Pray, girl. That's what I do when I have no idea which direction to go. I don't think there's anything wrong with a date, but only you know if that will cause more harm than good."

"See, that's just it." She leaned across the table. "I want to go out with him so bad, I can't stand it. But I *know* I'm not good enough. It would crush me if he became disgusted with me."

"And what if he doesn't, Belle? Would you throw away a chance at happiness for something you 'think' might happen?"

Belle bit her lip. That's exactly where she got stuck. How was she to know if it would happen? *But what if it does?*

"Here's a thought," Nina continued. "Tell him about your past, and then see if he wants to date you."

"Uh…he knows I was married."

"Does he know what that guy did to you?"

"He suspects."

"And he still wants to date you? See, go for it."

She smiled, but inwardly, her nerves quaked. Micah suspected she'd been abused, but she never brought up the adultery issue. Didn't want to bring it up. When should that enter into a conversation? Before the date? After the date? Or when you decided to be exclusive?

Nina started talking about the baby. Belle tried to follow along, but her mind wouldn't stop the onslaught of questions.

"What if the date is awful?" she blurted out. "How will we work together?"

Nina blinked at her abrupt interruption. A smile slowly slid into place. "I think you're not going to be satisfied playing the 'what-if' game. Go out with the man and let your brain rest."

"Sorry," she mumbled sheepishly. "He's just always in my head. I hear his laughter, his whistling when he's in a good mood."

"Girl, you got it bad. I suggest you go find him and end the misery."

"Find who?"

Belle's mouth dropped as Micah asked the question, looking much too good in a peacoat and jeans. Did she conjure him up?

"Hey, Micah, we were just chit chatting." Nina struggled to slide out of the booth. "Why don't you take my seat."

"You sure? You look like you need to rest." Concern creased his brow as Nina continued to rub her belly.

"No, I'm good. I'll talk to you two later." She wiggled her fingers at Belle and walked away.

Micah gestured toward the empty seat. "May I?"

"Sure," she squeaked. She cleared her throat and then paused. *What do I say?* "How was your New Year's?"

"So-so. Watched some football and relaxed. You?"

*Dreamy.* Which was quite literal. She'd daydreamed about going out with him. "Oh, it was relaxing as well." *Lord, please don't strike me down for that lie. I'm sorry.*

"Got any plans today?"

"Haven't thought past my stomach. You?"

"Same," he said with a grin lighting up his face.

Belle sighed.

"Something wrong?"

"No, just..." she shrugged. She didn't want to lie and didn't want to explain what her emotions were going through.

"Belle, would you like to go out sometime?"

"Like a date?" she squeaked.

"Like a date."

❦

*Oops. Did I just jump the gun, Lord?* Micah searched his heart but felt no discord. Instead the words, *it's time,* seemed to echo in his heart.

*Thank goodness.*

He'd hate to have to rescind the offer because of a slip of the tongue. He watched an array of expressions cross Belle's face. Surprise, interest, and finally regret settled on her face. His heart dropped. Had he been wrong? Was she not as interested as he?

"Micah, I don't think I'm the kind of girl you need." Regret softened her voice.

"So, all this time you've been pretending to be a Christian woman who loves helping people feel better?"

Her mouth parted in surprise. "No, of course not."

"Then go out with me. You can't tell if you're the right one unless we put it to the test." He grinned. Would it cover the fear of rejection hiding beneath his strained smile?

"We're coworkers. Isn't that a no-no?"

"How else do people meet?" He gave a mental shake of the head, remembering how the guys said the same thing to him.

She swallowed. "It's not that I don't want to—"

"That's a relief. I was beginning to wonder."

Belle laughed. "You're distracting me."

"No, I'm trying to get you to say yes. Should I get on my knees?"

"At The Pit? Everyone will know our business before we can even place our order."

"I'm sure they already do, Belle. I've never eaten here so many times. Don't get me wrong, the food is great, but I know how to cook. I come here hoping I'll run into you."

"Really?"

"Really."

A flush bloomed in Belle's cheeks as Dee walked up, notepad in hand. "Girl, say yes; you know you want to."

Micah chuckled. Thank goodness for friends' interference. Embarrassing at times, but their hearts were in the right place. He looked at Belle. "You ready to order?"

"Yes." She gave Delaney her order, and then he placed his.

Delaney winked at them. "I'll butt out now." She chuckled as she walked away.

Micah stared at Belle, pushing down the maddening urge to ask her out again. *Don't push, don't beg. Let her come the rest of the way, Soup.* He cleared his throat. "Did you enjoy Christmas dinner?"

"I did. Your parents are nice."

"Thanks. They said the same about you."

Her lips twisted. "You've told them about me, huh?"

Suddenly, he didn't need his jacket for warmth. He slid out of it, trying to stall before answering Belle. She stared at him expectantly, laughter turning her eyes into a rich brown.

"Okay, so I may have talked about you."

"Your dad told me to go easy on you."

"Please tell me you're joking."

She shook her head, her cheeks lifting high with suppressed laughter. "I told him I'd try."

He groaned. "There should be an age limit on how long your parents can embarrass you."

"At least your parents want to be involved in your life. My mother couldn't care less."

"Come on, I'm sure that's not true."

She spun her fork around, sighing out loud. "I wish."

He loved how she always twirled her utensils when she got nervous. Made him suspect he wasn't the only one unsure of what to do with all the feelings roaming inside. He reached over and stilled her hand. "I care."

She blinked rapidly, squeezed his hand, and then let go. "Thanks."

"Food's ready." Delaney appeared out of nowhere, setting their plates down. She looked back and forth between them, curiosity shining bright. She opened her mouth and paused. "Um, enjoy."

"Thanks, Dee," Belle said.

"Should I say grace?" Micah asked.

"I'll say it."

His eyebrow quirked in surprise. He'd always been the one to bless their food. Belle bowed her head, and he quickly followed suit.

"Heavenly Father, thank You for this food. Bless the hands that prepared it, and may it provide nourishment for our tummies. And Lord, please guide Micah to a restaurant with people who don't know us for our first date."

A grin split his face. "Amen." He paused, eyes roaming over her lovely face. "I'll be sure to get us away from the grapevine."

"Appreciate it." With a grin, she popped a spoonful of mac n cheese in her mouth.

Today was turning out to be a better day then he could have ever imagined.

*Thank you, Lord.*

## 17

Somebody needed to come up with a more descriptive word than nervous. The jittery sensation made her hands shake and her heart race way beyond the emotion beyond being just nervous. *Petrifying works.* Going out with Micah would either be the best thing since the proverbial sliced bread or fall into the worst-date category.

And it wouldn't be his fault.

Belle's fingers shook as they attempted to remove the plastic garment bag. After Micah had asked her out, she went back to the boutique she visited with the girls. This time she came home with a dress. The green cap-sleeved dress fell fluidly, glimmers of reds and browns streaking through. Now that she had started buying clothes other than scrubs, she couldn't keep away from color.

She quickly donned the dress and then some emerald, strappy heels—gorgeous and closed-toed. Of course, wearing a dress in January might give her a chill, but at least she would look date-worthy.

Once the shoes were on, she grabbed her lip gloss. The shimmering maroon color would be the only enhancement she'd allow. It was the most color she'd put on her face since Garrett had tried to rearrange the features. Funny how odd it seemed to have her lips sparkle with color. Would Micah think it strange or appreciate the effort she made?

Belle admired the pair of earrings she made the other day. After finishing another scarf, she'd been bored and had pulled out the jewelry kit without giving it much thought. They had been quite easy to make. A sterling silver hook, green orbs on a rope chain, and she had a new pair of earrings. She inhaled, slowly exhaling as she sent up a prayer, while staring into the mirror. For once, she wanted a full-length one. It had been one of the things she tossed in her purge to be more Christian-like.

*Lord, please help me decide if I should wear these or not. It's been so long since I've worn a pair, I'm not even sure my piercings are still open. I pray that You would keep my eyes on You and not puffed up in vanity. In Jesus' Name.*

"Amen," she whispered.

The ring of her cell phone broke her concentration. She grabbed it, frowning at the caller ID screen. *Unknown* flashed across the screen.

"Hello?"

Nothing.

"Hello?"

Belle glanced at the caller ID which showed the call was still in action. "Hello?" Nothing. She shook her head and hung up the phone. If it was important, they'd call back.

Making a decision, she put the earrings in, one at a time. Perhaps she would only use jewelry for special occasions. No need to be done up every single day. At least not for her. She didn't want to fall in the trap of her past vices.

Thankfully, she simply felt pretty and not borderline egotistical. She grabbed her clutch and her coat out of her closet. Micah said he would arrive at noon to pick her up. She couldn't imagine where he could possibly be taking her so early on a Saturday. She knew they were planning on going to dinner, but where on earth did dinner start at noon? Perhaps he needed a little time to drive them out of the Maple Run gossip range. If that were the case, then she would be more than happy to accommodate the early time.

*More time to spend with him.*

Stomach flutters kicked into high gear at the thought. Her cell rang again, interrupting her moment of stressing. *Unknown* flashed again. Who *was* this?

"Hello?"

Silence reigned. Apprehension slowly shadowed her nervousness. An image of Garrett's looming body appeared in her mind. "Who is this?"

*Click.*

Belle stared at the phone. Before she had gotten out of the hospital, she received prank calls from Garrett, at least that's what her lawyer had stated. But, there was no way it could be Garrett now, right? He was in jail and she had changed her cellphone number. It wasn't listed on any social media sites, and every effort had been made to ensure she couldn't be tracked. It had to be a prank caller or a horribly bad connection, right?

Fear skittered up and down her arms, leaving a trail of goosebumps. She wanted to run into her room and huddle underneath the covers, until the perceived threat went away. Instead of cowering, she prayed, asking the Lord to give her peace of mind. It would do no good to be looking over her shoulder the whole day. She wanted to enjoy her time with Micah.

*Speaking of which.*

She glanced at her phone to check the time and smiled when a knock sounded at the door at the same time. *Great minds.* Exhaling, she opened the door...and stared. Micah wasn't wearing a coat. The way his white dress shirt hugged his arms and the way the gray vest covered a well-toned chest mesmerized her.

*Talk about drool-worthy.*

A slow grin lit his face, dragging his goatee up, which only added to his appeal. "You look beautiful," he said.

"You clean up pretty nicely too, Mr. Campbell." Pretty nice was an understatement. She still wasn't sure if her breath had come back.

"Ready to go, Ms. Peterson?" Micah held out his arm, crooked at the elbow.

"Definitely." She slid her arm through his. A shiver of awareness shimmied its way through her at their close proximity. "Where's your coat?"

The corner of his eyes crinkled. "In the car. I had the heater blasting so it would be warm by the time I got to your place. I got too hot."

*I'll say.* She nodded primly, trying to keep her thoughts under control. "Makes sense."

He opened the passenger car door, bowing at the waist. She chuckled at his antics. Micah had a way about him that pulled a laugh from her. She was grateful the awkwardness of a first date didn't seem to be present. Her mind had already spun from her nerves as it was.

She waited until he buckled to ask the question that had been on her mind since he told her to dress up. "So, Mr. Campbell, where are we going?"

He waggled his eyebrows. "The ballet."

§

Micah loved the way Belle's eyes widened in delight. She clasped her hands together with excitement.

"The ballet? Really?"

"Yes, ma'am." He backed out of her driveway and headed towards the road that led out of town. "I figured Washington D.C. would be far away enough from the prying eyes of our town."

"I *love* the ballet. Then again, I've only been once, but still."

He laughed as she practically bounced in her seat. Seeing her this animated was almost as intoxicating as the gorgeous view she offered when she first opened the door. He hadn't been prepared for the dress, earrings, and hint of color on her lips. He'd gotten so used to seeing her in scrubs or jeans. Even the Christmas festival outfit hadn't hinted at how truly exquisite she could look. He tried to keep his eyes focused on the road instead of taking her in. She probably had no idea just how gorgeous she was. "Well, I'm glad I picked something you like."

"And something far away." Her grin had an impish tilt to it.

*Focus, Campbell, or you'll crash.* Micah turned back to the road. "Happy to help out." He paused, then started speaking. "Are you—"

"Did I—"

Belle laughed when they tried to speak at the same time.

"Go ahead," he offered.

"Did I tell you I'm getting baptized in a few weeks?"

His eyes immediately diverted from the road. "For real?" At her nod, he continued. "That's awesome!"

A shy smile turned her rosy lips upward. "Thanks. I'm excited for this step. Do you remember when you got baptized?"

"I do." He'd been down range...what the military types called deployments. "I was in Iraq and didn't want to come home without doing so." He didn't mention he was afraid to come back in a casket.

"Wow. I can't imagine that experience. Did anyone film it?"

"The chaplain assistant did. I gave it to my mom, since she couldn't be there to witness it."

Belle scrunched up her nose in concern. "Was she disappointed?"

"No. She'd been trying to get me to make that step for years. She was so grateful I finally did it, that she didn't mind the fact she missed it. I think my dad was a little hurt though."

"Do you have a close relationship with them?"

"I do. I've been lucky. I try and visit them at least once month.

My mom says holidays don't count, so I saw them twice last month." He glanced at her quickly before turning his eyes back to the front. "What about you?"

"No. My mom divorced my dad when I was young. I haven't spoken to him in years. I think he was so happy to be away from her he didn't look back."

The matter-of-fact tone hit him in the gut. Why wasn't Belle upset that her father had abandoned her? He'd be crushed.

"And my mom has been married more times than I can count since then. We don't agree on a lot of things, so we don't talk."

"At all?"

Belle shrugged. "It's been almost six months since the last time I reached out to her."

"I'm sorry." The platitude fell from his lips, but he truly had no idea what else he could have possibly said. He reached over and squeezed her hand. Micah quickly let go, hoping she would see the sincerity behind the words.

"It's okay. It no longer hurts, and my life has been better for it."

"Has it really?" He winced, wishing he could recall the words back. He did want to know, but he could have taken a gentler approach.

Belle tilted her head to the side. "Oddly enough, yes. I no longer have someone telling me how I'm failing at every turn. Do I wish our relationship was better? Sure, but I don't believe it will happen and agonizing over it won't help."

"Maybe you should try and talk to her again." He thought of how his father had said they seemed to both carry baggage. He knew Belle had some, but it seemed she had more than he realized. Had he jumped the gun asking her out?

"I'll pray about it."

He nodded. "Best thing to do."

"Can we change the subject to something lighter now?" She chuckled. "I thought first dates were supposed to be superficial."

He shook his head. Only Belle would be so forthcoming when

dodging a question. "What would you like to talk about, Ms. Peterson?"

"What's your favorite color?"

"Gray."

"Really?" Incredulity raised her voice an octave. "Isn't that depressing?"

"I happen to know I look quite debonair in the color."

Her laughter reverberated through the vehicle, and the tension of the previous conversation faded away. Micah would love to get her to laugh like that more often. Belle had her fun moments, but seriousness seemed to hang around her like a shroud.

"Well, you certainly look handsome tonight."

"Thank you. But it's nothing compared to you. If I knew you'd look like this out of scrubs, I probably would have shaken in my shoes the first time we met."

Her eyebrows rose in amusement. "Instead, you looked in the face of a woman with no makeup and held back the tears."

A bark of laughter escaped his lips. "Not at all. I assumed you knew you looked good without it and figured you probably had an ego to match your good looks."

"Oh, really? Now we're getting to some fun date revelations." She twisted in her seat, hands folded in her lap. "What else did you think about me?"

"Uh..." His collar suddenly felt too tight. "I may have thought you were a little rude. Then Mimi said how lovely and friendly you were, and I figured you had split personality disorder."

Belle's shoulders shook with suppressed laughter. "Good to know."

"But now..." He grabbed her hand. "Now, I want to know everything about you."

"Not much to tell."

"Oh, I'm sure the opposite is true. Those who are the quietest often have the best stories." He looked over and saw a strained smile cross her face.

## 18

She was a fool. What had possessed her to imagine she would ever be good enough for Micah Campbell? Last night's date had been wonderful. From the moment he picked her up, ushering her to his vehicle by the crook of his arm, to the very end. His cologne had called to her, daring her to rest her head on his shoulder, but that wasn't something Belle felt she could do on a first date.

And the conversation!

She sighed aloud. It had been endless except during the ballet, which had been spectacular in its own right. Everything about the date had shown her what a great guy Micah was. The gentle manners, like holding the doors and letting her order first, had melted her heart. All of it made her heart trip a little bit closer to the edge of falling in love. And when he placed a simple kiss on her forehead, her heart had fallen to the floor in a puddle of hormones.

Nothing on their date had been too fast or too slow. The man was a master of first dates. So, why did she wake this morning feeling wretched?

Because she knew the truth of her past would collide with the hurts of Micah's past. He told her she was a new creation, but he didn't know her past. Besides, a man that good didn't want a woman like her. Who would?

Sure, she had plans to be baptized, but that would only esteem her in the Lord's eyes. What Micah saw was a false representation. How did the old saying go about a pig? Well, that's what she was. Months of being a Christian couldn't erase her past.

*How could I ever be deserving of Micah, Lord? We're unequally yoked.*

His wife had cheated on him.

She cheated on her husband.

Two polar opposites could not meet in the middle. Going on a date with him had only confirmed the absurd thought that her past wouldn't matter. She sighed, covering her face with her hands. Hot tears pushed at the back of her eyelids, threatening to spill out.

Belle tilted her head up, never removing her hands, as she fought to keep the tears back. Instead, they slowly slid down the sides of her temples and into her hair. "I want to be new, Lord. Truly new." The words burned in her throat, breaking free in heartache.

"How can I do that when my past faces me? Every. Single. Day? Is there no future for me?"

Silence met her ears. Always the silence.

Her cell trilled, interrupting her pity party. Okay, so not everything was quiet.

"Hello?"

"Belle?"

"Hi, Dee."

"Hey, I was wondering if you'd like to go dress shopping with me?"

*Ugh, not again.* She didn't want the lure of another dress. "I don't know. Church will be starting soon."

"Not today, silly." Humor laced Dee's words, hinting at held-back laughter. "Saturday." Dee's voice dropped. "I need to find a wedding dress."

"Oh my gosh! I would love to go with you." Who didn't like weddings? Plus, she wouldn't have to worry about pretty things calling out to her. She could focus on Dee and be a supportive friend. "Wait a minute, wouldn't you rather someone else go with you?"

"It'll be another ladies' gathering. Nina and Nikki are coming as well."

"Oh, then in that case, I'd love to. When's the wedding?"

"Valentine's Day."

"Dee! That's next month."

"I know, but I hate shopping."

Belle shook her head. She couldn't imagine not liking it. Well, now that she didn't, it wasn't as far a stretch as she thought. "Hopefully they'll have one in your size."

"That's what Nina said."

"She's right. It takes them forever to alter."

"Well, I already have someone in mind to alter it if I do need that. I thought we could go shopping and then catch lunch afterward. Sound good?"

"Perfect." Now she had an excuse just in case Micah asked her out again. Her heart pinged at the thought.

They hung up, and Belle got out of bed. It was time to get ready for church. Part of her wanted to sleep in, but since she just talked to Dee, now she'd have to go to church. But what would she do if Micah sought her out?

Without another thought, she redialed Dee's number. "Hey, can I sit next to you in church?"

"Uh oh, bad date?"

"I plead the fifth."

Dee snickered. "Sure, girl. Sit by me, but just know you owe me a recap."

"Thanks, Dee."

She tapped her cell against her chin. It was wonderful having a friend she could call on. Never in her thirty years had she had that before. And right now, she needed one.

She made a calculated choice when picking out her clothes. Her black slacks, in wide-leg fashion went well with her green, tunic top. Last, she added clear lip gloss. For some reason, she felt the need to make Micah realize this was who she had to be. Not a woman worth dating.

Satisfied with her appearance, Belle grabbed her things and headed for the car. Snow flurries drifted down as she buckled up. The weatherman said it wasn't going to stick. So far, their winter had been relatively snow-free. She turned the radio to the Christian station. There was nothing better than hearing uplifting music on the way to church. She could only hope and pray that the sermon would pull her out of this funk. Having a painful and tainted past seemed incredibly unfair. It would have been fantastic if God could wipe it as clear as He could forgive. Her mind refocused as Natalie Grant came on the radio.

The woman's voice made her think of angels singing. She glanced at the info screen on her radio to look at the title of the song. "Clean." *Appropriate, don't you think, Lord?* It was like the song was made for her, for this time, to lift her up.

Sure, God could see her as beautiful and wonderful since He made her. But what about others? As she turned into the church parking lot, her heart began to pick up speed. The sincerity of the song's words tore through her, ripping her into shreds with the truth.

God could make her a new person. No matter her past. And right now, that was all that mattered. Not the possibility of a relationship with Micah. Not the clothes she wore, hoping others would see the new being. Just her and God.

He'd made her whiter than snow. Turned her mourning into praise.

Tears streamed down her face as she sang along, arms raised in worship. As the notes of the piano rang out, she laid her head on the steering wheel, sobbing. She wanted everyone to look at her as God did. To not see her past. To not see the harm and hurt she'd caused.

A knock sounded on her windshield. She wiped her face with her sleeve before turning to see whose attention she'd captured. Micah and Dee stood there.

*Why, Lord? I don't want him seeing me like this.*

With a sigh, she pressed the down button to her window.

"Belle, what's wrong?" Micah asked.

"I can't talk right now." Her throat felt raw as she pushed against the rising tide of sadness. Tears slipped free, running down her face. At least she didn't have to worry about ruining her makeup.

"Do you want me to get the pastor?"

"No," she shook her head. "Micah, please go away."

Hurt flashed in his eyes as he righted himself, standing to his full height.

"Unlock the door, Belle," Dee said.

She complied, but it didn't block the waves of hurt coming from Micah. *See, I did it anyway. Upset the one man I truly don't want to hurt.*

※

*What just happened?*

Delaney had just driven off, effectively preventing him from finding out why Belle was sobbing her beautiful eyes out. Angst filled him as the need to fix whatever ailed her went unfulfilled. He kicked at a rock in the parking lot. How was he supposed to go into church and pay attention when he wanted to jump in his SUV and follow them?

He ran a hand down his face, frustration peaking.

"Where did Dee go?"

Micah turned, noticing Luke for the first time. "She just left with Belle," he motioned over his shoulder.

Luke's brow furrowed. "Why? Is something wrong?"

"Belle was crying. Didn't want to talk to me." He gulped. "Delaney talked to her and then they drove away. I have no idea what's going on."

"I'll call her." Luke pulled his cell phone out his back pocket. "Darlin', where are you? Uh huh...right here....okay, I'll tell him."

*What were they talking about?*

Luke slid his cell back into his pocket. "They're at Delaney's. She said Belle will be fine and that you should go to church."

"That's it?"

"Sorry, man." Luke clapped his hand on Micah's shoulder. "Some women need to work things out for themselves before they share."

A groan tore from his lips. "Ugh."

"Yep," Luke said with a wry grin. "At least you know she's not alone."

"True. Wait," he stopped walking. "Does that mean she's suicidal? Should I go talk to her? Does Delaney know what to do in these cases?"

"Soup, chill out. I just meant you didn't have to worry about Belle crying by herself."

"She's *still* crying?" How many tears could one woman possess?

Luke laughed. "Man, you got it bad. I seem to remember you telling me to trust in God. Seems like you forgot your own advice."

"Yeah, well, you never made Delaney cry."

"Are you sure you made Belle cry? She could have gotten a bad phone call."

"Then why wouldn't she tell me?"

"Maybe she thought you'd try to fix it."

He stared at Luke. Was his friend crazy? *Of course,* he would fix it. That's what you did when you had a problem. "Crusoe, we're supposed to fix problems. We're men."

"Now, if that isn't some Neanderthal-type talk coming out of your mouth, I don't know what is." Mrs. Williams placed a hand on her hip, blocking them from the church's entrance.

"Hi, Mrs. Williams."

"Don't 'hi' me, Micah Campbell. I can take two guesses as to who you think needs to be fixed. So, let me do you a favor. Let a woman vent or hoot and holla if she needs to. We don't want all problems fixed. Sometimes, we just need to vent."

*That made no sense whatsoever. What was the purpose of complaining if you didn't want to fix it?* Fortunately, he had the good sense to refrain from saying that out loud. He didn't need Mrs. Williams getting more riled up than she already was. "Yes, ma'am."

She smiled and then turned to Luke. "Where's my sweet girl?"

"With Belle, ma'am."

"Hmm, I take it she's the one who needs to vent. Are they coming back?"

"Probably not, ma'am."

"Luke, you ever going to call me Mama like everyone else?"

"February 14th."

She chortled and headed inside.

Micah laughed at the bemused expression on Luke's face. "You're not going to call her Mama, are you?"

Luke shuddered. "I'm terrified to. But I can't call her Mrs. Williams either."

"She's not that scary."

"Ha, that's because you aren't marrying one of her children."

Micah laughed. Couldn't argue with that. He followed Luke into the sanctuary, thankful for a few moments of levity. Still, he couldn't help but wonder what was going on with Belle. What could make her cry like her heart had been broken? He was sure she'd be just as excited to see him as he had been to see her. Last night's date still lingered in his memory.

He hadn't asked her for another date when he dropped her off last night, but he planned to this morning. That was until he saw her leaning on the steering wheel, the sound of her sobs coming through the windowpane. He sat down in the pew and bowed his head as everyone got ready for the service.

*Lord, I have no idea what's wrong with Belle, but please flood her with Your perfect peace. Please break down the barrier that's preventing her from talking to me. I want to be the one she can confide in. I know that's not necessarily realistic considering we've only been on one date, but I thought I earned her trust. Was I wrong?*

He sighed. *No matter. Please just dry her tears and heal her hurt. Amen.*

## 19

Belle stared blankly at the table as reality faded and scenes from the past came forth.

Carter was nothing like Garrett. He was kind, considerate, and good looking. Okay, so sure, once upon a time, she thought Garrett had the same traits, but that was before she saw his true self. She smiled as Carter opened the car door for her.

Garrett wanted her to schmooze him, aka do "whatever it takes to get him to sign the deal." Those were the words Garrett commanded when he'd picked out her outfit for tonight. This was the first time he didn't plan on attending a business meeting with her. Belle wasn't sure how being alone with Carter would ensure he signed the contract with her husband but knew she couldn't go home without some type of assurance. Thankfully, Carter was easy to talk to.

"So, Carter, how did you meet Garrett?"

"We go to the same club." At her blank expression, he continued. "Golf."

"Oh, right." *Garrett played golf?* What else didn't she know about her husband? "Is that how you guys began talking business?"

"Sure is. It seems almost a common factor at the club. Most of us are businessmen, so that's where the conversation tends to end up."

"Are you going to work with him on a permanent basis?" Did that sound like genuine curiosity instead of fishing for hints?

"It depends." He grinned and slid a hand up her pencil skirt.

Nausea rolled in her gut. The implication wasn't lost on her. Men had always flirted with her and often times she responded in kind. Especially when attending a business function with Garrett. A commodity—all she'd ever be to him.

But this was the first time Garrett pushed the boundaries. She wasn't sure what Carter did, but no matter how nice he was, she didn't want to do what he was suggesting. Did she?

Garrett's face flashed in her mind. Would he be angry if she came home now? She turned back to Carter. "Depends on what?"

He squeezed her knee. "I think you know."

Ugh. She was afraid she did. "Are you saying you'll do business with my husband if..." She couldn't bring herself to finish the sentence.

Unfortunately, Carter had no qualms about choice language and finished it for her. He grinned as if committing adultery was an everyday venture for him.

*What do I do?*

Only, no one was there to answer her. Garrett had beat her once for not sealing a deal, but this was different. Carter was asking for a lot more than flirting. Plus, Garrett had always showed possessiveness, so she couldn't have understood him correctly.

*"Belle, if you don't get him to agree to a business deal with me, don't come home."*

Belle blinked and looked around. Something had pulled her from the past and back to the present. Right in the break room of Dr. Kerrington's family practice.

"You okay, Belle?"

She looked up and saw Mimi standing in the doorway. "Yes, sorry. My mind was a million miles away. Did you need something?"

Mimi sat down. "Just wondering what's going on between you and Micah. He looks like a lovesick calf, and you look like a frightened jaybird."

Belle forced a laugh. "A calf and a bird, Mimi? Are you sure the cold isn't getting to you?"

"All right," she held her hands out. "You don't have to talk to me, but I think there is someone you should be talking to."

Anyone but Micah. She knew exactly what Mimi meant by lovesick. Every time she passed him in the hall, he looked at her as if she just stole his dog...or parrot in his case. "Mimi, I..."

Again, the woman held a hand up to halt her words. "I really don't want to know the particulars. But I do want to say that Micah Campbell is a good man. He doesn't deserve the cold shoulder, no matter what happened." With that, the older woman rose and left the room.

Belle slid her head into her hands. This was exactly why she should have never agreed to a date. The atmosphere was full of tension as they tiptoed around each other. As for talking—she snorted—not likely. What could she say? *Sorry, Micah, you're too good for me, so stop looking at me like that?* Yeah, that would really go over well.

A knock sounded at the door. She lifted her head, and her stomach dropped to her toes. Micah leaned against the doorway, looking glorious in his dress shirt and slacks, his head gleaming under the office lights.

"You okay?"

She nodded wordlessly, even though it was a lie. Would she ever be okay?

"Can I come in?"

"Yes."

He sat down across from her, his eyes searching her face. She tried to meet his gaze but couldn't face him. She looked down, staring at his tie, trying not to notice the muscles beneath.

"What's going on, Belle? Did I do something? Say something wrong?"

She shook her head. If she willed hard enough, maybe the tears would refuse to fall.

"Didn't you have a good time Saturday?"

"I did," she rasped out.

"Then what happened?" he asked softly.

"I'm not good for you, Micah."

He lifted her chin with his fingertip. Her head nestled into his palm before conscious thought entered. A tear slid down her face. Slowly, his thumb wiped it away. "I thought we already went through this."

"But our date made me realize how wrong I was to believe that a person's past doesn't matter."

"It doesn't, Belle."

She offered a sad smile. "Every time someone says that, fate proves them wrong."

"Do you believe in God or fate?"

"Micah..."

"I'm serious." And judging from the hot look in his eyes, he really was.

"God."

"Then your past doesn't matter. He says it, and I'm reiterating it."

"But you're only human. How do you know I don't have some skeletons that will scare even you?"

"Because I don't care."

"Sure, you don't. Right now, you're living in the glow of a good first date. But when that wears off, when we're left with our true selves, you'll regret acting so rashly."

"Really? Do you think so little of me? Do you know how long I've wanted to ask you out? But I didn't. I took my time.

Not because I wanted to, but because God told me to be patient."

His words took her breath away. She struggled for air and words. "Maybe you should have waited longer."

"Nah," he shook his head. "According to you, I shouldn't have bothered. We could have something beautiful, if you let the fear go and hold onto me and your belief in God instead."

Tears slipped down her cheeks. Was he right? Was it just fear talking? She believed in God with all her might. Had to, because if she didn't, then there was no hope for her perishing soul. But to trust another person when she knew what faulty creatures they were—was absolute torture. "I want to."

"Then please do," he whispered. "I can't make you want a relationship. I can't conquer your fears. Only you can do that. All I can do is promise you I'll still be here when you finally leave the past in the past." He held out his hand. "Take a risk with me, Belle, please."

Micah stared at Belle, his heart pounding in his chest and echoing in his ears. Would she take hold of his hand or leave the office?

Her eyes scanned his face, then dropped to his hand. She picked her hand up and then stopped.

*Please, Belle.*

His heart pleaded with her, but he refused to say anything. He'd already said enough. Begged for her to take a risk. She wasn't the only one afraid, but he refused to live in fear. If God had Belle in mind for his future, then he'd cling to that truth.

She wiped her face with the edge of her sweater. "Okay." She placed her hand in his and squeezed.

Relief poured through him as his shoulders drained of energy. He held her hand up to his forehead, thankful for her trust. He had no idea what was in her past, but he could only plead and pray to the Lord that when she finally told him, he'd fulfill his promise and remain in her life.

*Please, God. Let my love endure her past. Let my love endure trials and tribulations. Just let it endure.*

Micah stood and pulled her to her feet. He guided Belle around the break room table and into his arms. She held on tight, nestling her head against his chest. A sigh of rightness left his body. He rubbed his hand over her short bob, trying to soothe her aches. "We'll be just fine," he whispered.

After a minute, she pulled back. Her eyes still held a hint of turmoil, but not as much as when he first walked into the break room.

"Ready to go back to work?"

"Yes, I suppose I'm done hiding."

He chuckled. "Thank goodness. I wouldn't have made it through the remainder of the day. Your silent treatment packs a terrible punch."

A frown furrowed her brow.

Taking a gamble, he spoke up. "Did someone physically hurt you, Belle?"

"What?" Her eyes widened, and she stepped out of his arms. "Why would you ask that?"

"There have been little clues here and there." He slid his hands into his pockets, trying to still his nerves. He'd wanted her to come clean. To trust him enough to share her past, so he could show her it didn't matter. As usual, his patience reserves had emptied faster than he'd intended.

She wrapped her arms around her middle. "I thought my behavior was pretty normal."

"It's not abnormal to distance yourself from men, if they were the ones who hurt you."

A shaky breath slipped from her lips. "My ex-husband had a long list of expectations. Unfortunately, I never seemed to get it right."

Anger burned his gut. No one should be subject to that. *No one.*

"At first, I was too shocked to even object." She maneuvered her hair behind her ears, her hand shaking with nerves. "I tried to tell my mom, but..." She shrugged.

"Your mom didn't care?" Disbelief colored his words.

"She's not very maternal."

"She's your *mother*." The words came out clipped as his jaw clenched with anger.

"By blood." She cupped his cheek. "Don't be upset, Micah. My mother is who she is."

He grabbed her hand and placed a kiss in her palm. "I'm sorry you were hurt."

"Me too." She opened her mouth, then closed it.

"What?"

"Nothing," she said with a shake of her head. "That's enough for now. I'm going to see if there's a new patient."

"Okay."

She squeezed his hand and then left the break room.

He sat back down, resting his head in his hands, as his elbows propped him up. *That's enough for now.* What more could Belle possibly have to share? He'd seen the shadows come back and the wall slide right back into place. The thought of her ex-husband doing something unspeakable—for what else could he think? — made his blood boil. Belle was precious in God's eyes and therefore worthy of the utmost care.

*Lord, I pray she knows I'd never hurt her. That I would seek to treat her as You command us to: with love.*

The words poured out of his soul as he continued to pray. Finally, he stood and headed for the front. If there were patients, he'd need to be prepared. Doctor Kerrington saw scheduled patients while he handled the walk-ins. It was a good system and worked out well. Mimi looked up as he took his seat in the little alcove.

"Belle just took a walk-in to room ten."

"Thanks, Mimi."

"You guys good now?"

He chuckled. "Yes. All's well."

She slid a hand over her forehead. "Thank goodness. If the tension got any thicker, it'd rival the Virginian humidity."

"We're not as bad as the weather, Mimi."

Mimi raised an eyebrow, placing her hands on her hips.

"All right, maybe just a bit."

"Ha, a bit, he says. Go on, Micah Campbell, before you make me regret my words."

With a smile, he sauntered down the hallway.

## 20

Laughter rang in the air as they waited for Delaney to come out of the dressing room. Belle held her stomach as Nikki did an impression of Mrs. Williams. The woman in question shook her head.

"I know I can be a bit much, but I'm not that scary," Mrs. Williams said.

"Please!" Belle clapped a hand over her mouth. "Sorry, didn't mean to say that aloud."

Mrs. Williams rolled her eyes.

Nina snorted. "Mama, you had me terrified when I first met you and it only got worse."

"Well, how was I supposed to know you weren't the villain?"

"See, who thinks like that?" Nina asked, pointing to her mother-in-law.

Belle snickered. "At least Micah's not one of your kids."

"He may not be, but think of me as his surrogate mama." She pointed a finger at Belle. "I'm watching you, young lady." Mrs. Williams emphasized her point by motioning with her fingers.

They all laughed again.

Mrs. Williams gasped, her eyes widening and mouth dropping open.

Belle turned and saw Delaney enter the waiting area. She wore an ivory gown with layers and layers of ruffles. It was a bit much in her opinion.

"Dee, sweetie, you look gorgeous," her mother whispered.

Delaney's mouth twisted. "I look ridiculous. Look at all these ruffles! I look like I'm on top of icing."

Nikki's shoulders shook as she glanced downward. Belle had to stifle her own laughter.

"Dee, girl, if you don't like it try another one," Nina suggested.

"But she looks gorgeous," Mrs. Williams cried out.

"No, Mama, that's not the one," Nina countered.

"Fine. Try another one on."

Delaney sighed and headed back with the attendant.

Belle met Nina's gaze over the top of Mrs. Williams' head. The other woman shook her head and grimaced while signaling toward Delaney's parting back. Belle nodded in agreement. That last dress was not the one. Delaney had looked miserable and that wouldn't do on what was supposed to be the happiest day of her life.

A pang hit her in the center of her chest as Belle remembered her own wedding. She'd worn the best gown money could buy and walked down the aisle knowing she was making a mistake. Her mother had tried to assure her that Garrett would take care of her every need.

She snorted under her breath.

Delaney returned, this time wearing a mermaid-style dress. The dress was form fitting, flaring out at the bottom. Her eyebrows raised in question. "What do you think?"

"Nah."

"No."

"Next," Mrs. Williams said.

Delaney laughed. "Good, I don't like it either." With that, she stepped down from the podium and headed for the back again.

Mrs. Williams glanced at Belle. "Are you next?"

"Next for what?"

"Marriage, Belle." Mrs. Williams rolled her eyes in exasperation.

"Uh, no. We've only been on two dates."

Nikki clapped her hands. "You guys are so cute together."

Nina nodded.

"Well, just remember Micah's not getting any younger," Mrs. Williams stated. "And you're thirty, right?"

"Mama," Nina whispered harshly. "Please leave the poor girl alone."

She lifted her hands as if to say "what?"

Belle shook her head. Mrs. Williams was a hoot. Thank goodness she wasn't related to Micah. *Such a blessing, Lord.* Besides, she adored Micah's mother. The woman had been kind to her at Christmas, and his father was pretty hilarious.

Belle turned at the sound of movement and stared.

Delaney walked out in a pale pink, sweetheart-neckline gown. The straps were in the shape of lace flowers. The sheath overlay gave it an ethereal look to it.

"Oh, Dee," Belle whispered.

Mrs. Williams began crying as she held a hand over her mouth. Delaney's smile widened as she took in everyone's response. "This is it, y'all."

"Definitely," Belle agreed.

"Girl, you're going to knock his socks off," Nina said.

"Oh man, I'm going to cry," Nikki wailed.

They all got up and took turns hugging Delaney as she posed in front of the mirrors. Belle smiled as she sat back down. She wouldn't have missed this moment for the world. Delaney made a beautiful bride. The pale pink color of the gown seemed to add an extra glow to her beautiful brown skin.

"I can't wait to see your groom's face," Belle said.

"Me either." Somehow, Delaney's grin stretched further. "He'll love it."

"Because he loves you," Mrs. Williams said. "I'm so glad you get a second chance at happiness."

Belle smiled as Mrs. Williams hugged her daughter. She still couldn't believe that Delaney was a widow. The woman seemed like she had a great life. Yet, her husband had died almost four years ago, and Luke had felt responsible. He'd come to Maple Run to make amends and ended up falling in love.

*Please bless their marriage, Lord. Let them have happiness until Your return. And maybe even bless me with a little bit of happiness, too.*

෴

Micah whistled as pulled his V-neck sweater down over his belt. Belle was coming over for dinner. Now, he had a chance to show off his culinary skills. He hadn't been joking when he said he could cook, but that didn't mean he had Dwight or Luke's skills. Thankfully, he could follow directions and could keep food from burning and make it edible. He grimaced, maybe he should have taken her out for dinner instead.

"Ding-dong," Noodles croaked.

Micah frowned, looking at his watch. He hadn't heard a door bell, but if Noodles said 'ding dong' then he must have missed it.

He hurried to the front door and then smoothed his hand down his chest one last time. *Here goes, Lord.*

Belle stood there in jeans and a jacket. She smiled up at him. "Hey."

"Hey there." He took her hand and guided her into his home. "Let me get your coat."

"Sure." She slipped out of it, so he could hang it on the coatrack.

She had on a cute, green, cable knit sweater.

"I'm beginning to think green's your favorite color."

"It is." Her cheeks pinked up. "And you do look good in gray," she said, pointing to his sweater.

"I try," he joked. He took her hand. "Come on, I'll give you the tour and introduce you to Noodles."

He showed off the kitchen, the spare bedroom, and then headed for the living room. Micah tried to view it from her eyes. He knew the black furniture was masculine in its build, but hopefully the gray accents made it homey and not dreary.

"I leave Noodles' cage in here. Sometimes, he goes out in the aviary, but it's kind of cold right now."

"Tell me about it. I can't wait for spring."

"Likewise." He stopped in front of the cage. "Noodles, meet Belle. Belle meet Noodles."

"Pretty lady."

Belle chuckled, the sound reminding Micah of a wind chime. "Smooth talker, huh? Nice to meet you, Noodles."

His feathered friend dipped his head. "Pretty lady."

Micah rubbed his chin. "He does say more than that."

"I'm sure."

"Do you want me to take him out of the cage?"

"Sure."

He opened the cage and held out his arm. Noodles gripped it with his talons, all the while staring at Belle. He tilted his head to the side. "Pretty lady. Hi, pretty lady."

"Hi, Noodles."

"African grey's can be a little territorial, so I'll let him scope you out. If he tries to come near you, you'll know he likes you."

He stood there for a few minutes, telling Belle about his bird. She watched raptly, chuckling at his antics. Finally, he put Noodles back in his cage.

"Hungry?"

Belle nodded.

"Noodles hungry."

"I'll get your fruit."

He took Belle's hand, guiding her toward the kitchen. Now that she was in his home, he didn't want to let her out of his sight. It seemed like it took them awhile to get to this level of comfort. Somedays, he still waited for the other shoe to drop. She never shared more about her past, but he knew it was there, waiting to be aired.

*Lord, please let me be an attentive listener.*

After serving Noodles, he washed his hands. "I didn't want to start dinner until you got here." He motioned for her to sit at the barstool.

"What are you making?"

"Shrimp scampi."

"Mmm."

He grinned as he poured some olive oil into a skillet. "Don't worry, I already put some bread in the oven."

"How did you know I like bread?"

"You always get a roll or two when we go to The Pit."

Belle chuckled and shrugged. "What can I say, carbs are my best friend."

"Well, this carb will be dressed with butter and garlic."

"Sounds great."

He tossed the shrimp into the skillet while watching Belle. His heart was full. Seeing her in his home, did him in. He could imagine coming home to her every day.

*Whoa, marriage?*

Okay, so not right this moment, but marriage with Belle... perhaps it wasn't as scary as he imagined. After all, she was nothing like Denise. Being with Belle would be worth the fear of another failed marriage. Without a second thought, he rounded the island, cupped her face, and placed his lips gently on hers.

She whispered his name softly against his lips, and he increased the pressure. Her arms twined around his as he took his time telling her how much she meant to him. Slowly, he withdrew his lips, still holding her.

He rubbed her bottom lip with his thumb.

"I'm glad you did that before we had garlic."

Micah laughed and laid his forehead against hers. "I really, *really* like you."

"And I like you."

## 21

Belle grinned with excitement. She couldn't believe it was time to get baptized. As soon as she woke, her spirit seemed to sing with delight. Worship song after worship song flooded her mind as she sang along. Thankfully, she didn't have a roommate or a husband to object. Not even a pet to cover its ears. Today, she wanted to feel the powerful blessing of being dunked in water.

The only problem was her hair. When it got wet it curled up tighter than a corkscrew. It would be a bear to blow dry and straighten, but it would be worth it. She put on her black clothing to ensure propriety. When the pastor first mentioned it, she'd been a little disappointed. She'd always thought people got baptized in white to symbolize purity and a new life.

Oh, well, God knew what was happening no matter what she wore.

Belle stared at her cell phone. For a second, the overwhelming urge to call her mother pressed upon her. She hadn't spoken to her since she called from the hospital begging her to visit. And her mother never showed. What could she even say? *Hi, I'm getting baptized?*

Her mom would keel over in shock or simply hang up the

phone. Still, her hand reached for the phone and had her number pulled up before conscious thought kicked in.

"This is Carol Anderson, to whom am I speaking to?"

Belle rolled her eyes. No matter how many times her mother remarried, she always kept her maiden name. "Hello, Mother."

"Well, long time no talk, daughter dear. You just up and left and didn't bother to tell me?"

An objection rose as tears beckoned to fall at the injustice. She *had* tried to tell her mother, but Carol Anderson didn't listen unless it involved her own agenda. Belle inhaled, sending up a prayer before she spoke. *Honor thy mother and father.* "How are you, Mother?"

"That's all you have to say after all this time, Belle?"

"Yes. I...I missed you." She stared at her cell. Had she really said that? Oddly enough, it rang true.

"Really? I must talk to my phone carrier. Apparently, they've failed to show me the many messages you left saying so."

*Why?*

Why did she have to make everything so difficult? Lord knew she was trying, but her patience was wearing thin, fast. "I'm sorry. I didn't think you wanted to hear from me."

"Then what changed your mind?"

"I...I, um—" okay, she needed to just spit it out. "I'm getting baptized, and I wanted you to know."

"Baptized?" Her mother spoke each syllable as if she'd swallowed rancid milk.

"Yes, Mother. I've accepted Jesus Christ as my Savior. Getting baptized is the next step." Maybe she should have called her mother a few days beforehand and invited her. Except, she never thought she'd pick up the phone and call her mother in the first place.

"Hmm, so you've found religion?"

Belle shook her head. She could practically see her mother using air quotes. "It's more than that. It's a relationship."

"I see. You threw away a real relationship with a man who could provide for you, beyond our greatest hope, and traded him for an imaginary man in the sky?"

"Mother..." What did she expect? Her mother refused to believe Garrett was capable of destruction. She had refused to see Belle in the hospital, even though the police had shown photos of the damage he'd wrought on her face.

"I would have preferred the non-existent voicemails as opposed to this...this nonsense. Anderson women make their own destinies. We don't answer to some supposed higher power."

"He makes everything better."

"I'll take your word for it. You can even say a prayer for all I care, but please, don't call here anymore."

A tear slid down her face as her cell phone screen showed her mother had hung up. Once again, she'd reached out and received silence for her efforts. What was the point of Scriptures if people didn't respond in kind?

*"Doing the will of God from the heart; with good will doing service, as to the Lord, and not to men."*

Belle sighed as the words echoed in her head. She had to want to do good because God called her to, not because she expected the same service. When it came down to it, she'd be judged by her actions alone, not on what others did to her. She rubbed her head, battling the tears.

"Lord," she whispered, "don't let her take my joy. I'm not getting baptized to get accolades and well wishes. I'm doing it because I want to draw closer to You. I *need* to be closer to You. Please help me block out the noise preventing me from drawing closer to You. Help me to remember why I was happy to wake up this morning."

No matter what happened between her and her mother, she still had the Lord. He was a father to the fatherless, at least that's how she thought the Scripture went. She wasn't perfect in remembering them all nor what book of the Bible they were in, but she wouldn't let it stop her from trying. It was time to do what God called her to do and stop looking for her fellow man's approval. Doing that had led her down the wrong path before. A path she had no intention of returning to.

It was time to get washed by the water and join the body of Christ.

§⋅

The sanctuary buzzed with light-hearted chatter and laughter. Micah looked around, noting the extra faces present to cheer for those who were making the next step in their faith journey. Unfortunately, no one from Belle's immediate family would be here. He knew it bothered her, had seen it in her eyes when he wished her luck.

Thankfully, the gang had shown up with balloons and flowers. Even his mom and pop had come. Times like these, he was thankful for his friends, family, and church. No one should be baptized without a cheering section. Of course, he knew that wasn't always the case. Some people were the only saved members in their family. But it still killed him that her family hadn't shown. He knew her relationship with her mother wasn't good, but this bad? Bad enough not to show up for a momentous occasion?

*Lord, I pray that Belle doesn't let the lack of her own family sour her moment. May she feel the Spirit and Your presence as she takes this step. Amen.*

He took a seat as the pastor began speaking. Pastor Brown remarked how they had five people who would be joining the church family. Micah gave a mental shake of the head. He'd always found it a little strange when pastors said that. In his eyes, a person joined the family as soon as they professed the Lord Jesus Christ as their Savior. But maybe they just wanted to highlight the momentous occasion.

As Belle took center stage, in the baptism pool, he leaned

forward. The look of excitement on her face mesmerized him. He wasn't close enough to see her eyes, but he could imagine they fairly sparkled with joy.

"She shines, son." His Pop smiled with his eyes as he whispered to Micah.

"She does."

"Then don't fear for her."

He nodded and faced forward in time for the pastor to begin speaking.

"Belle Peterson, have you professed to accept the Lord Jesus Christ as your Savior?"

"I have accepted Him as my Savior and expressed my need for Him." Her voice rang steady and clear.

"Then on the profession of your faith, I baptize you by the power of the Father, the Son, and the Holy Spirit," Pastor Brown proclaimed. He dipped Belle back and under the water, then brought her up.

Micah stood to his feet, clapping and cheering for Belle. A wide grin covered her face as she made her way out of the pool and to one of the assistant pastors, who held a towel. He sat back down, trying to pay attention to the next four members, but his mind was still on her. Finally, he heard a rustling sound and saw Belle walking down the aisle toward him.

For a moment, he could envision her in a white gown with flowers in her hands and a smile just for him. He blinked, realizing she really did hold flowers. Right, they were probably from the pastor's wife. She gave flowers to every new baptized believer.

"Congratulations," he whispered. As she sat next to him, he placed a kiss on her cheek.

"Thank you. Did you record it?"

"Couldn't, too nervous." He pointed to his father. "Pop did it for me. Plus, I think the tech crew is recording it for everyone."

"Oh, good."

"Want to go eat after church?" His stomach had started making noise while the last person got baptized.

"How about I cook you and your family lunch?"

She was inviting them to her place? He wanted to throw a fist in the air. Finally, she trusted him enough to enter her domain. "Sounds great," he said with a suppressed grin.

"Good. I can't cook that well, but I can heat up some food like you wouldn't believe."

He chuckled, trying to keep his voice down. "You're going to get me in trouble laughing."

"So, I shouldn't tell a joke?"

"Please no," he groaned. "You can save them for lunch."

"I just might do that."

*I'm sure you will.*

❧

Micah sat in the little alcove. The office was extra quiet with Belle out sick. He prayed it wasn't his fault. After all, they had sat on his deck for a couple of hours talking Wednesday night. No, this Friday seemed to be mourning her absence.

"Uh, Micah, there's a gentleman here to see you." Mimi looked at him, wrinkles lining her forehead and her eyes crinkling in wariness.

Micah looked up from a patient's file, his mind focused on Belle.

"Micah?"

"I'm sorry, Mimi. Did you say a patient is looking for me?"

"No," she said, shaking her head.

A pharmaceutical rep maybe? Then again, why didn't she just say that? He eyed her, looking for some clue.

She had a look of unease.

"Is it business?"

"He said, personal. That's all."

"Ok-ay. Put him in an empty room and I'll join him."

After saving the current file, he locked up his laptop. He headed down the hall toward room three, where Mimi said she had escorted the gentleman. Who could it be?

Micah double tapped the door, waited a brief second, and then entered. A man about three inches taller than him and a couple of shades darker stood, his arms folded across his chest. Controlled fury were the best words to describe him.

Caution snaked up his spine. "Can I help you?"

"Are you Micah Campbell?"

"I am." *Seriously, who was this man?*

"I'm Garrett Peterson, Belle's husband."

His breath whooshed out, and he reeled backwards. "Husband?"

A proprietary gleam darkened Garrett's black eyes to coal. "Yes. I've just arrived in town to talk some sense into her. She seems to think our relationship is over." He dropped his hands and slid them into his pockets. "I saw you two together. You could imagine my shock."

Like the kind he was experiencing right now?

"You seem like a reasonable man. So, I'm sure you wouldn't want to be party to anything unsavory."

Nausea rolled into his gut, threatening to push past his esophagus. *Belle was married?* "I had no idea."

"Of course not. Belle's a little conniving." Garrett flashed a grin that was all teeth and no warmth. "She'll say and do anything to get what she wants."

Micah sat on the nearest chair, rubbing his forehead. The woman Garrett described was not the one he knew. Then again, what did he know? He had no idea she was still married. Her "husband" said she would lie, but that didn't sit right. He licked his lips, knowing he had to proceed cautiously and remember what Belle had told him. "I thought you two were divorced."

"Minor blip."

His eyebrow involuntarily arched. Okay, something wasn't jiving. If this guy was the one who hurt Belle, what's to say he'd be honest? "So...you *are* divorced."

Irritation flashed on his face. "Like I said, minor blip. Besides, I thought your type didn't believe in divorce."

"My type?"

"Christians," he sneered.

How did this man know he was a Christian? But besides... "There are some biblical grounds for divorce."

"Such as..."

"Adultery is one." The one he used to end his marriage with Denise.

"Ah." A Grinch-like grin stole across his face. "I guess then I did have grounds for a divorce."

"What?" Micah's jaw dropped.

"Your precious Belle cheated on me." Garrett shrugged his shoulders. "But that's okay. She was lonely, and I'm willing to overlook it now."

Belle cheated on *him*?

That couldn't be right. That wasn't the Belle he knew. The one who devoted herself to Christ and cried tears of joy at her baptism. "You must be mistaken."

"Oh, no. There was *no* mistaking that."

*Lies.* He had to be lying. His heart picked up speed as he remembered the certainty in which Belle spoke in the past. *You don't know what's in my past.* If what her ex said was true, then—

"I don't understand why you would tell me this."

"I figured you might want to back off."

"Back off," he repeated slowly. "Back off, so that you can restore your relationship with a woman that cheated on you?" He was slow, but he wasn't that slow. Why would he want Belle? Warning bells rang like crazy in his mind.

Garrett's fist clenched at his sides. "Look, just leave us alone. I need to talk to Belle and she won't hear me out with you fawning all over her."

"Yeah, that's not going to happen." He cocked his head to the side. "Do you even have a right to be near her? Don't you have to stay what...like 250 feet away?"

A tick appeared in his jaw.

*Bingo.* It was a calculated guess, but apparently a good one. Belle had to have a restraining order against him. Probably lying about her cheating on him as well. "You need to leave. Since this is her place of work, you have no right to be here."

"We'll see about that." He shoved past Micah and left the room.

The relief he felt was short lived, because his gut instinct told him this wasn't over.

*Belle!*

He needed to call her, or better yet, go by her place and make sure she was okay. He raced toward the front room. "Mimi, I need to leave. Emergency. If you don't hear from me in ten minutes call the police. I'm going to Belle's."

Her eyes widened in shock and she gave a short nod.

His vehicle zipped past the streets of Maple Run. *Lord, please keep Belle safe. Please don't let Garrett figure out where she lives.* He didn't want to imagine what would happen if Garrett got to her first. In no time, he parked in front of Belle's apartment building. He unbuckled his seat belt, flinging the door open and shut. As he raced up the sidewalk, Micah said a prayer for her safety. His heart pounded in his throat, adrenaline and fear upping the beats per minutes to a frantic pace.

Quick knocks brought no answer. "Please, please, please," he murmured. He knocked again.

"Coming," Belle called out.

Relief poured through him, but his heart wouldn't stop pounding. He needed to see her, make sure she was okay.

Belle opened the door, wearing sweats and a red nose. "Hey, Micah. What are you doing here?"

"Checking on you." He swiped a hand across his forehead. "Do you have company?"

"No," her brow furrowed. "Why would I have company? I'm sick, remember? You shouldn't even be here."

"Your ex-husband hasn't been by?"

"What?" She took a step back. "Why would you ask that?" She folded her arms across her chest.

"He came to the practice looking for you."

Belle's eyes grew wide, darting back and forth. "Oh, no," she whispered. She whirled around and headed for the back of her apartment.

Micah entered, closing and ensuring the door was locked, then raced after her. Slowly, he entered her bedroom and stopped. The sight before him stunned him. He watched as Belle grabbed clothes from her closet and threw them into a suitcase.

"Belle, honey, what are you doing?"

"I need to leave. It's not safe." She paused and met his gaze. "You need to leave."

"Belle," he laid his hands on her shoulders. "It's okay. You have a restraining order."

"Not for the state of Virginia and if he knows where I work, you can guarantee he knows where I live. I have no desire to end up in the hospital again." Belle froze as if realizing what she just said.

*Hospital?*

## 22

Belle's stomach dipped as nausea rolled up like a sand storm. Beads of perspiration popped along her upper lip. She hadn't meant to blurt out her secret like that. Of course, she wanted to tell Micah over dinner or some point in time not so chaotic.

The look on his face was enough to send her reeling for the bathroom. She had no time to decipher what it meant before her stomach contents ended up in the toilet. Heave after heave had her leaning closer to the porcelain throne. What should she do?

There was no way she could stay here, but the look on Micah's face begged to differ. She owed him an explanation. After cleaning herself up, she headed back in her bedroom. Micah sat on the edge of her bed with his head in his hands.

At the sound of her footsteps, he looked up. Lines creased his forehead. "You okay?"

She shook her head.

He held out his hands, and she placed hers in them. Gently, he guided her to him. "Why didn't you tell me?"

"You said my past didn't matter, and I wanted to believe it." She shrugged. "So, I didn't say anything."

He lowered his head against her stomach. "But how can I protect you if you don't share this?"

Her heart ripped in two at the anguish in his voice. How could she tell him she deserved the beating Garrett dealt? She lifted his head up. "It's not your job to protect me."

"Like—" he clamped his mouth shut, effectively stopping his words. His nose flared as his chest rose with each breath. "If anything ever happened to you..."

"Shhh," she placed a finger on his lips. "I need to tell you something, and I need you to listen. Don't interrupt or I won't finish."

He nodded, eyeing her cautiously.

Belle stepped out of the comfort of his arms and stared into the eyes of the man she'd come to love. "I cheated on my husband."

"What?" He croaked.

"I cheated on Garrett. When he found me, he went into a rage, and beat me up. I had to have surgery to piece my wrist together." She rolled up her sleeve and showed him the scar. Now was not the time to hold anything back. "They removed my spleen and I had to receive a few bags of blood." She looked down at the floor, hating the shocked expression in his obsidian eyes. "The district attorney's office pressed charges without my knowledge. When I came to, they informed me that a restraining order had been put into effect. They put him in jail without bail and a few weeks later I received divorce papers. I signed them and started looking for a place to start over."

Belle stared at her socks. What was Micah thinking? The thought terrified her to her core. She didn't even want to look at him for fear she'd see disgust in his eyes. A tear dropped onto her sock, then another. After a couple of more tears dropped, Micah's hand came into her line of vision. He gently lifted her chin up. She squeezed her eyes tight, refusing to look him in the eyes.

"Belle."

She shook her head.

"Look at me."

As she did, more tears fell freely.

"Why did you do it?" His gaze searched hers.

Did she really have to tell him? Wasn't it bad enough already?

"Tell me."

"He..." She licked her lips. "He wanted to secure a business deal."

Micah's eyes widened. "What did he tell you to do?"

"Micah," she jerked her hand trying to sever the contact between them. Instead, he wrapped his other hand around hers.

"All of it. I want to hear all of it."

Belle gulped and then told him the entire tale. Her words came quick as she rushed to get the sordid details over with. She didn't want him to know, to look at her differently than the cherished woman of God. But she couldn't deny him the truth.

"That son of a—" Micah turned away before he uttered the last word.

She'd never seen him this angry. "Micah, it was my fault."

He whirled around. "Are you serious? That man gave you an ultimatum. Who treats their wife like some commodity?" He slashed his hands through the air. "No. I'm not placing the blame at your feet."

"I do."

"Belle," he groaned. "You can't blame yourself for that."

She nodded vigorously. "I can, and I do. I'm a grown woman capable of making my own decisions. I chose to cheat and that's something I have to take responsibility for."

Micah shook his head vehemently. "No. I don't agree. That man used you. Manipulated you. Messed with your mind. You probably believed you had no choice. No, just no. I don't agree." He moved forward, gently cupping her face. "I understand why you didn't tell me. But thank you for telling me now."

Tears filled her eyes. How had her truth brought him closer to her? "I'm sorry," she breathed out.

"There's nothing to be sorry for, honey. I'm not mad at you at all. If anything, I'm mad at him."

"Really?" She gulped, trying to understand what was happening. "You don't hate me?"

His eyes softened. "I could never hate the woman I love."

"Oh, Micah," her head dipped in relief. "I love you, too."

"Thank God." He leaned forward, placing a gentle kiss on her lips.

She wound her arms around his neck and kissed him back. Relief had her sagging in his arms. *He doesn't hate me!* She thought for sure he'd hightail it without a backward glance once her past caught up to her.

*Garrett!*

She gasped and stepped back. "We need to get out of here."

Micah glanced at his watch. "I need to call Mimi. She was going to call the police if she didn't hear from me in ten minutes. I'll call their office number and give them a description of Garrett. You may not have a Virginia restraining order, but you do have one for your home state. That's got to count for something."

In awe, Belle watched as Micah took control of the situation. Somehow, her past hadn't tainted her future or her relationship with him. Here he stood, calling Mimi and the police. For her. Belle Peterson, former adulterous. No, child of God. *Mind blown.*

*Thank You, Heavenly Father, for giving me Micah.*

# EPILOGUE

*Valentine's Day*

Belle squeezed Micah's hand as Delaney repeated the vows the pastor had stated. Her friend looked stunning and absolutely in love. The couple chose not to have any bridesmaids or groomsmen. Instead, Preston and Philip stood as witnesses and participants in the ceremony. She sighed and laid her head against Micah's shoulder.

When she'd bowed her knees in repentance, she couldn't have imagined that a man could love her, knowing her past. She knew that God had wiped her slate clean. Knew He had made her into a new creation. Still, she never thought that *people* would offer the same grace or love. Falling in love with Micah had finally cemented the idea that she was beautiful on the inside and worthy of love by the saving grace of Jesus Christ.

And now that Garret was no longer a threat, she could truly live the abundant life God so richly offered. The local sheriff's office had informed her that Garrett had several outstanding warrants for his arrest due to some shady business deals he'd orchestrated. Now, he remained behind bars awaiting a trial that all but guaranteed he'd be sentenced to a life behind federal bars.

Couple that with her new Virginia restraining order, Belle could finally breathe easy.

Life was as close to perfect this side of heaven that it could get.

Micah placed a kiss on her forehead as the pastor proclaimed the newly married couple, "Mr. and Mrs. Luke Robinson." She stood, clapping in celebration for the couple. *Lord, bless them with a lifetime of memories and love. I pray they're blessed with old age and grandchildren.*

She couldn't imagine the courage it took to fall in love after losing a husband. Then again, when the right man came along...

Micah held out his hand and she walked down the aisle with the rest of the people who had gathered together for this special wedding ceremony.

"You okay?"

"Mmm hmm." She offered a smile. "Close to perfect."

"I'll say." His eyes gleamed with love and admiration.

Belle paused, moving to the side so others could pass by. "I just want to thank you again for not giving up on me."

"Never." He ran a hand down her cheek. "You deserve to be loved and cherished."

"I know that now."

"And I'll always be around to remind you."

It wasn't a proposal, but she didn't need one to know how much he loved her. He'd loved her through her pain, through her past, and fully in the present. One day, she knew he'd make a declaration to love her as a husband, and until then, she would happily date this man of God.

OTHER BOOKS IN THE MAPLE RUN SERIES

*Buying Love*

*Finding Love*